AF432322

Captive of the Stars

Ellen Russell

For Tim

Chapter 1

Carina ran headlong into the forest, her threadbare jacket snagging on the half-dead branches as her lungs labored to suck in the thin mountain air. She didn't dare look back to see if the soldier still chased her, and couldn't hear any sounds of pursuit over the rapid beating of her heart and her own gasping breaths. Her synthi-wool cap caught on a jagged branch and came off, tugging her braid free from where it had been pinned up.

Then she heard the terrifying sound of heavy footfalls. She glanced behind instinctively — inwardly cursing herself, knowing it would only slow her down. One of the Varusians soldiers, in full armor and helmet with a clear face shield, wasn't far behind. She let out an involuntary shriek, and pushed herself to run even harder.

She dodged between two close trees, then vaulted over a small boulder that lay in her path. She stumbled as her boot caught in a hole in the dry dirt. She nearly went down, and just managed to grab the flaking bark of a tree to keep herself upright. Her right boot slipped off in the process, leaving her tattered, gray sock exposed, but she couldn't stop. She pushed on, trying to avoid the worst of the sticks and rocks on the ground.

The Varusians had attacked without warning. She'd been riding the rickety transport up to the titanium mines along with other Seuturan citizens who lived in her colony, chatting away with her friend Bryn. They had been just a few kilometers from reaching the mines when the unimaginable happened: a Varusian ship descended, and soldiers poured out.

Carina had heard of the Varusians, of course. Everyone had. They were the people from the only other habitable planet in system. The rumors said they were a war-mongering, barbarian people, decorated with the technologically advanced illusion of culture. It seemed the rumors were true, but the Seuturans and Varusians had held a tentative truce for decades, never tangling in one another's affairs. What had changed?

Her breathing was labored already. As hard of work as her body was used to in the mines, she seldom had to run. She frantically scanned the forest ahead of her. When the attack started she had tried to pick the direction that would take her back toward the colony, further down the mountain, but she wasn't sure where she was now. She didn't usually venture into the forest and she was a long way from the colony. Had she gotten turned around? The forest sloped downhill in front of her, but that could still take her far away from home. And even if she made it, what good would it do? They had a local peacekeeper to deal with minor matters, but he wouldn't be able to do anything against a battalion of armed Varusian soldiers. And while there was planetary military, it could be hours before they could mobilize and send aid.

Maybe she could get far enough away — far enough to make the soldier lose interest. She wasn't sure how far he would pursue her.

She wasn't sure of anything right now. She was a simple miner. She had no chance in an actual fight. She was fortunate the soldier hadn't shot at her already.

She didn't understand why they would be after her or anyone else on the tram. They were nobodies. She was a nobody. When her work shifts were over, all she did was tend her tiny rows of potted herbs and spend time with her few friends. And the rest of the workers were just like her. No one important rode the tram if they could help it.

Her feet slid as she curved around a tree to avoid its dead branches. She had to throw out her arms to keep herself upright. She saw a small clearing ahead and she forced her legs to move faster, ignoring the pain in her thighs and lungs. Abruptly she was slammed into from behind, and the steel-like arms of the soldier wrapped around her. As she fell to the ground, the grip around her tightened, and she felt herself being twisted around. They hit the ground hard, but the soldier took the brunt of the impact.

Carina struggled, desperately trying to free herself from the solid arms holding her. The grip loosened as the soldier shifted to get up from under her and she took advantage of the moment to scramble away on her hands and feet. She could hear the soldier rise and follow her, his footsteps almost casual as he approached her.

She tried to stand, but her feet slipped on the leaves on the ground and she landed against a tree trunk. She spun and saw the soldier still taking his time, walking towards her. Through the clear faceplate she could see his piercing green eyes and sharp jaw. Her hands desperately reached for anything she could use to fight back. Her fingers closed on loose leaves and twigs before tightening down on a rock. The soldier stopped, standing over her. She had nowhere to maneuver. He knelt down, his hands reaching for hers. As he grabbed, she moved under his arm and swung her hand holding the rock at his helmet. He let out a short curse, but managed to dodge her swing, and the rock glanced off. With a flip of his wrist, he deftly secured her two hands, pinning them to the ground, and squeezed her arm until she was forced to drop the rock.

She squirmed beneath him, trying to push herself up to escape. But his grip remained firm, his well-muscled body easily pinning her against the tree trunk.

Terror siezed her. She panicked, twisting wildly, and tried to do anything to get out of his hold. But he was too strong. It felt as though her thrashing accomplished nothing — he didn't seem remotely bothered.

After several ineffective moments, she slowed her struggle. The futility of it reached her brain just as her adrenaline started to taper off. She found her face centimeters from her attacker's chest. His black armor was shaped with the contours of muscles. Intricate etchings covered the material with pictures, flowing over one another, making them tough to distinguish.

Before she could get a better look at them, her attacker's head shot up, pulling her attention away from his armor. She saw an intense look take over his face as he stared out into the forest. She tried one more time to break free from his grip, but even distracted he held her with ease.

"Two minutes," he said, then rose, pulling her with him. It took her a moment to realize he must be talking into a comm device she couldn't see. He reached into a pouch at his side, and pulled out a strand of twisted, metallic fiber with a large, cylindrical joint. Even as she struggled he twisted it expertly around her wrists with one hand while gripping them tightly, though not painfully, with the other. The fiber tightened, holding her hands fast.

The soldier grabbed the cylindrical joint between her wrists and pulled her along, back toward the way they had come. She stumbled over the dirt and rocks with her one remaining scuffed boot and other thinly-socked foot.

"Wait!" she said, yanking her hands as hard as she could. Her braid had partially come loose at this point, several portions falling in front of her face. When her bootless foot hit a particularly sharp rock, she stumbled and nearly fell.

Before Carina could blink, the soldier spun around and grabbed her, then hefted her up and threw her over his shoulder. The impact knocked the air out of her, and she found herself staring down the back of the soldier to the rocky ground below, the loose strands of her hair brushing her face.

"Put me down!" she said, trying to kick him. He said nothing, but pinned her legs and increased his pace, jogging now, back toward the transport.

She made a fist with her bound hands and pounded on his back, but all she did was ineffectually connect with his armor. She couldn't imagine what this Varusian wanted with her, and she didn't want to. Whether death or a worse fate awaited those who were being taken, she didn't know.

Soon she heard voices, a few shouts, and the increasing roar of machinery.

"We good?" the soldier holding her asked, slowing his pace.

"All set. Locking up now," came another voice. She could see the lower half of a soldier in an identical set of armor next to her captor. She tried to twist her head for a better look but her awkward angle prevented her from seeing anything more.

He strode further, and the low thrum of engines began to reach her ears. Then she saw metal below her, and she panicked.

"No, no!" she said, kicking wildly. The noisy engines and the metal floor meant they were boarding a ship, and a ship meant they were going away — far away from here. Far away from the planet. She couldn't get taken from here. Not away from home and everything she knew.

The world spun, and she wasn't sure if it was more from the realization of what was happening or from the soldier depositing her onto her feet on what was clearly the ramp of a ship. She would have slumped to the floor if not for him holding her wrists.

"No time to waste, Buttercup," he said, tugging her up the ramp. She pulled back, her one boot skidding on the textured metal surface, but he kept pulling her along, ignoring her struggles.

"What is going on?" she said, her voice sounding far weaker than she had intended. She had wanted to sound forceful, to demand a response.

"Later," was all the soldier said, not even turning to face her. It sounded far gentler than she could have imagined a soldier to ever be, but it still had an iron will behind it.

They entered the ship proper, and he took her past a small cargo bay. Carina stumbled as she saw a large, barred enclosure full of people — *her* people — cuffed as she was, huddled together. The soldier didn't pause and she had to struggle to keep up and not fall over. The Seuturan people were all dressed in their work uniforms, a drab gray that hid the dust of the mines well. The uniforms were wrinkled and mussed like after a long day, even though they had just been heading up to the mine when they had been attacked. One man was fighting as two soldiers struggled to push him through the door of the enclosure, shoving him in with the others captive Seuturans. She saw many faces that were normally lively, if tired during a day's work, now just staring blankly, too shocked to even react. They were miners, not soldiers. She felt as though she were in a daze. Why were they taking them? And where?

The soldier continued to pull her along through the cargo bay. There was a constant, but organized, stream of activity all around them in the tight space. A group of soldiers to the right were breaking down what looked like a massive blaster and storing it in metal crates. Two others were locking the containment area with workers, including a weeping woman, inside.

They approached a set of metal stairs that ran along one side of the bay, flush against the bulkheads. Soldiers ran up and down the narrow space, boots clanging against the grip lines of the steps. The steps led to an upper area of the bay, a deck that extended out a couple meters from the wall.

The soldier was intent enough with wherever he was taking her that he wasn't paying attention to her. She jerked back hard on her wrist restraints before they reached the stairs, hoping against hope to get free, but the soldier kept his grip tight on her bindings. He turned and looked at her. Through the clear visor, she saw him raise an eyebrow and smile. He seemed more amused at her struggles than angry or upset. "Gotta go get strapped in, Buttercup."

Carina didn't know what to do. Her struggles seemed to not even register with him. Perhaps begging could work. Surely all Varusians couldn't be heartless barbarians. She began to plead, "No — let me go, please. You can't just—"

"No time to chat." He gave the cord cuffs a firm tug, then turned to head up the stairs, pulling her along. The pressure on her wrists was too much to even let her think of resisting.

He led her up the stairs, away from the other Seuturans. Another soldier greeted her captor and clapped him on the back. Carina received more than one curious look, but her captor didn't offer an explanation even to his fellow soldiers. She looked back over her shoulder, down at the containment area that filled the hangar packed with workers. Why wasn't she being put with them? She looked around. Soldiers everywhere were moving with a seemingly singular purpose, but no other captives. She was the only Seuturan outside of the cage that she could see.

The soldier pulled her through a hatch down a narrow passageway, and then past another hatch, which gave her a brief view of a group of soldiers settling into seats. The ship was higher quality than any she'd ever seen on Seutura, even in the nice newsvids — gleaming walls, floor, and ceiling, well-lit, and in seemingly good repair.

He abruptly pulled her through another hatch and Carina found herself in a room with two narrow rows of seats facing each other, mostly filled with armored soldiers.

"There you are, Ram. Was about to send an alert out," one of the other soldiers said. "Thought a local might have tried to smash your head in with a rock." He was strapped into one of the seats and had a deadly looking weapon held between his knees. All the soldiers were dressed in the same imposing armor, but each one had unique, intricate designs embedded in the black material. There were symbols and many other things she couldn't identify.

Her captor — Ram must be his name — grunted a laugh, then maneuvered her into one of the seats before she had a chance to react. She tried to push herself back to her feet, but he easily held her down. The seat was large, clearly meant to hold an armored soldier like those around her. She felt small in it, and even more frightened than before.

"One nearly did," Ram said, gesturing at her.

The other soldier laughed. But another with stern brown eyes stared at her and her captor. Through his faceplate, she could see his mouth twisted into a ridged frown. "Snatch and grab, Ram," he said.

Ram crouched down before her and began deftly buckling a harness around her. "I know," he said. He shot her a grin and winked. "Couldn't resist."

Her eyes welled with tears as he continued buckling her in, which she blinked furiously away. The sheer magnitude of her situation was still sinking in, but she would not be weak and cry. She'd had to be strong before — wouldn't have survived in a mining colony if she hadn't.

The soldier's face softened slightly, and he brushed some of her loose hair from her face. "Cheer up, Buttercup. You get to go on an adventure."

Carina looked at him, incredulous that he seemed so flippant. How could he joke at a time like this? She was being ripped from all she knew by a group of brutal soldiers. And he thought it wasn't a big deal. He rose and took the seat beside her, quickly buckling himself in.

"Delta group checked in," the stern soldier said into a comm device near his shoulder. His voice was steely cold. The hatch of the room slid shut with a hiss. He looked back over at her, then Ram. "Thekla is going to have your hide. Easy targets only, Ram. We're late to the rendezvous because of you."

Ram shrugged. "I'll handle it."

Her seat vibrated as the ship's engines powered up. Panic gripped her. She was stuck here with no way off the ship. No way to get away. Her hands were cuffed in a way where she couldn't even reach the latches to the harness. Around her, soldiers were chatting casually, even laughing. She shuddered as numbness threatened to overtake her. The lights dimmed briefly, and she must have inadvertently made a sound, because Ram reached over and clasped her hands in a firm, gloved grip. "Never been to space, Buttercup?"

She didn't answer as she felt the ship take off from the ground. The acceleration pressed her into her seat, and for a moment — just a moment — she was thankful for the seat restraints. She squeezed her eyes shut. Her chest felt tight. Never been to space? Of course she hadn't.

The average Seuturan never even had a thought of going to space. Only a handful of non-military had ever gone. The government had their research stations in system, even a decent size base on one of their moons. And there was a small fleet of ships on hand, though even those were more a necessity to transport personnel than to provide defense.

The ship continued its ascent and she opened her eyes. The soldiers around her just chatted on, far too jovially in her opinion. Then there was a brief jolt — she let out an embarrassing squeak — and then the ship went still.

Chapter 2

"ETA to the *Architeuthis*: seven minutes," a voice announced out of a comm speaker on the wall above the hatchway. They hadn't stopped, of course. They had reached outer space. She was still moving with unfathomable speed away from her home.

This couldn't be happening to her. *What* was even happening? Question after question flooded her head, but her mouth didn't seem to work at the moment. The absurdity of expecting answers while surrounded by the very soldiers who had invaded her homeworld prevented her from voicing her questions.

Seutura had to have some sort of contingency plan in place for this, right? Or would they retaliate? She cursed herself for her lack of interest in intra-system and planetary affairs.

Would the Seuturan fleet try an attack? How many ships did the Varsuian fleet have? Surely Seutura would try to get their people back, although she wasn't sure what the fleet could do besides shoot. At the moment, she debated what was worse — dying in the cold vacuum of space or being at the mercy of the Varusians.

She thought back to her short trip through the cargo bay. She hadn't seen her friend, Bryn, in the containment area. There had been too many people to easily tell if she was actually there or not. But what concerned Carina the most was that she herself wasn't in that area with the others. What had made this soldier take such a particular interest in her?

The ship lurched once more, throwing her against her restraints. She tensed again, but nothing else happened.

A signal sounded over the comm, and abruptly the entire room was moving as soldiers unbuckled and rose from their seats. There was a charged energy to the air, the sounds of laughter and of slapping one another on the back. Someone let out a loud whoop. *They* were *barbarians*, she thought with disgust. They had just taken dozens of innocent people captive and they were downright joyous about it.

The large, armored soldiers soon began filing out of the hatchway.

Her captor crouched down before her, startling her. She flinched back, but of course couldn't go anywhere. He reached up and twisted his helmet, and it slid off with a quiet hiss, fully revealing his face and tousled brown hair. In other circumstances, she would have thought him handsome. His hair was mostly closely cut, though a few strands hung down onto his forehead. He set the helmet on the seat beside her, then began unbuckling her crash webbing.

The stern soldier stopped just behind him. "I take it you're going to be dealing with her?"

Dealing with? Carina's blood ran cold. She didn't know what that meant, and she wasn't sure she wanted to find out.

"Look, you do have some brain cells left, Alex," Ram said, throwing a grin over his shoulder.

Alex growled, and Carina tensed. "I'll let Thekla know you won't be there for processing. He's going to have a conniption."

"Hmm. What else is new?"

Alex huffed, then stalked out of the hatchway. Ram finished unbuckling her straps. He held her cuffed hands and rose smoothly, pulling her to her feet.

"Please," she said, desperately trying to pull her hands away. The room was empty now, though noise echoed in from the rest of the ship. Ram frowned down at her boot-less foot. "I don't understand what's happening. Can you — what's going to happen to us?"

"Don't stress, Buttercup," he said, tapping her chin gently. He towered over her by a good fifteen centimeters at least, with his strong jaw and striking eyes adding to his imposing appearance.

"Stop calling me that," she said, pulling back as her anger rose.

His grin broadened and he grabbed his helmet from the seat, tucking it under one arm, but he didn't answer as he led her to the hatchway. Then he scooped her against his chest, up into his arms in one abrupt, smooth movement. Somehow he was still able to keep hold of his helmet as he carried her. He held her firmly, and her stomach dropped.

"Put me down!" She twisted, but his grip didn't loosen.

"You're missing a boot," Ram said. As if that was enough explanation. He began to stride through the ship, back the way they had entered.

"Because you attacked our transport!" she snapped. "I can still walk."

"No can do, Buttercup." Carina gritted her teeth. "Got-ta check out those wounds, and I don't want you getting more hurt on the way. Besides," he said, glancing down to give her a reproving look, "that other boot doesn't look much better than being barefoot."

"I wouldn't be hurt if it wasn't for you!" she said. Pro-voking the large, enemy soldier certainly wasn't the smart-est plan, but she didn't want to be carried around like a helpless damsel. She thrashed her still bound wrists, trying to free herself.

She felt a small victory as he loosened his grip on her as she swung at his face, but then she realized she was fall-ing.

It was only for a moment. He caught her again and stood back up, holding her almost in the same grip, but this time he had somehow managed to grab the cylinder holding the fiber around her wrists with one hand and was holding tight to it. It was uncomfortable, but bearable if she didn't struggle.

"Either this or over my shoulder. Your choice, Buttercup." He smirked, continuing his way toward the ship exit. She bit her tongue, resisting the urge to tell him exactly what she thought of his choices.

Then they stepped out of the ship and she was speechless for an entirely different reason.

The ship they had just been on was tiny in comparison. It was just a small shuttle, she realized, dwarfed by the enormous hangar bay they'd stepped into. Dozens of other ships, just like the one they exited, filled the bay. The wall behind them was simply a semi-translucent sheen of blue, and beyond it she could see the expanse of stars. More shuttles were still entering through the blue sheen and landing. The sounds as much as sights overwhelmed her — engines were powering down, people were shouting, and many prisoners were desperately pleading. The same charged energy she'd seen in the soldiers in the shuttle was amplified here.

The entire hangar was a flurry of organized chaos. Soldiers in armor like she'd seen already, and others in variations of armor and uniforms were herding people — all clearly Seuturan citizens. There had to be hundreds of them. Most had dazed expressions on their faces, which she knew likely mirrored her own. Several had clearly attempted to fight back, and were in far more restrictive restraints than she was. She saw a man with a leg in a brace and a woman bleeding from her head, both on floating stretchers being moved by what looked like medics.

Aggressive shouts rose above the cacophony of the hangar and drew her attention. It came from the ship beside them. She craned her neck, trying to see what was happening, and Ram's steps slowed. Captives were being led out, and it looked as though an argument was occurring between a Varusian soldier and one of the captive men.

The man's hands were restrained, but that didn't stop him. As he cleared the ramp, the man rammed his shoulder into the soldier, knocking him back a step, and then went for the holstered weapon on the soldier's belt. His fingers latched on and tugged the blaster out, but the soldier slammed an armored fist into the side of his head, sending him reeling. The Seuturan fell to the ground, blaster still somehow in his hand. Before he could raise it, however, the soldier was on top of him. Fists slammed into the captive's head, pounding it against the floor. The soldier kept it up for several seconds before finally rose and retrieved his blaster.

From the way the captive lay, Carina knew he was dead. Blood seeped onto the deck, and his neck was turned in an unnatural way. The soldier had killed him, when he could just as easily have disarmed him. Her heart stuttered, and she suddenly found it hard to breathe.

Her captor let out a curse, turning her away and picking up his pace as he brought her toward a large set of doors leading out of the hangar bay. The commotion of the fight died down behind them, but the hangar was still loud with activity. Her captor kept moving until they passed through the doors and her view of the hangar was obscured. Her breath still came in short pants.

"That shouldn't have happened," he told her solemnly, and she saw a tension in his face.

The captive shouldn't have resisted? Or the soldier shouldn't have killed him? Carina wondered which one it was, but didn't know if she really wanted the answer.

"Wait," she said. "Where are you taking me?" She realized she didn't see any other Seuturans being brought this way. She was being moved away from the rest of her people again — from the last thread to home and what was familiar.

"To get you cleaned up and have a medic take a look at your foot."

"But — I don't understand—"

"What's not to understand? Your foot is hurt, you need it looked at," he stated matter of factly. Someone in a dark blue uniform passed them and he greeted them, as if he had fully answered her question.

The corridor was calm compared to the bustle of the hangar, but still busy. The floor was a gray metal that was covered in a simple pattern of hexagons. The walls were gleaming white, and the ceiling seemed to glow, washing the entire hall with bright light. It stretched far into the distance, with doors and corridors stretching off on both sides. She couldn't comprehend how large the ship had to be. She'd seen vids of the insides of Seuturan transport ships, but they were tiny compared to this, closer in size to the shuttle that had brought her here than this massive ship. She felt as though she'd been whisked into another world.

How could the Varusians manage such a feat? She had heard the rumors, of course, that they were more warrior focused than Seutura, but she couldn't imagine the resources necessary enough to construct something of this magnitude. How much had they sacrificed to build it? Even if Seutura tried to attack it, they wouldn't have much hope against a vessel of this size. And, as the enemy soldier took her farther from the hangar, she wondered how she could get back with her people on this ship, let alone hope to escape alive.

Chapter 3

Ram made his way to the area on the *Architeuthis* that had been designated for processing the Seuturan captives. He inwardly cursed the impulsive anger he'd seen displayed from a fellow soldier in the hangar. Not that he didn't feel a burning anger inside himself — most of them did after what Seutura had done. But the fool should have known better than to act on it in a situation that was already under control.

The soldier would be disciplined, he knew, but he was sorry the Seuturan woman had to see that. Her face had paled even more than it already was. She had been scared to begin with — now she must be downright terrified. He wondered if he ought to say more to assure her, but decided against it. It's not like she'd believe him anyway, and he didn't want to overwhelm her with the details that would only marginally bring her comfort.

He glanced down at his captive. Her foot was bleeding — it didn't look too bad, but he wanted to get her checked out soon. He was rather appalled at the condition their drop group had found the miners in. He knew Seutura was supposedly a backwater civilization compared to Varus, but seeing it with his own eyes was quite a shock. This was just supposed to be a hostage mission, but maybe she was better off here than where she was.

He stopped at a hatchway and pressed the keypad beside it. The door slid open, and he stepped inside. The room was curved slightly, rows of hatches spaced along a back wall. Anca, one of the administrative staff on board, stood behind a tall metal desk, dressed in a neat, dark blue uniform. She was bent over a screen, but looked up as they entered.

"You're the first from your group, Corporal," she said to Ram.

"Special circumstances. Which room?"

"Just take one," she said, nodding toward one of the hatchways at the far end of the room.

"Thanks, Anca." Ram strode over in the direction she had indicated. He felt his captive tense up in his arms.

The room he brought them into wasn't large, but it had a bench, a computer unit on the wall, and two other hatchways. He set the girl down, then unlatched and unwound the cuffs. She shoved away from him as soon as she was free, and he hid a tired grin. It didn't make much difference — in a room this size, he could grab her easily, but at least she showed she still had some spirit left in her.

But he let her be and stepped over and tapped his authorization code into the computer unit. Out of the corner of his eye he saw her eying the hatch, but he ignored that. Even if he didn't stop her before she reached the door, she couldn't get very far. He pressed the button to the cabinet wall and turned in time to see her jump as it opened. Inside was an orderly pile of clothes and a pair of shoes.

"Bathroom's in there," Ram said pointing to one of the hatchways as he handed her the clothing. "Ten minutes." He went to sit on the bench.

She remained frozen for a moment. At first he wasn't sure if she understood. Under all the shock, it was possible she wasn't processing things properly. But then she looked as though she might argue. She seemed to think better of it, and stepped through the hatch.

Ram waited impatiently for the girl, arms crossed. She was probably plotting his death right now.

He had been impressed with her when he saw her escape the tram. She had smashed a cracked window to get out, and then helped one of the older ladies out first. She might have had time to escape if she hadn't. He had already been hard pressed to overtake her and make it to the extraction rendezvous — those extra few seconds would have made him even later if he had chased her, maybe forcing him to break off his pursuit. But for some reason he had pursued her, even knowing Thekla would have him performing diabolical training exercises for the next month. And then she'd had the gaul to swing a rock at him, helmet and all. This was going to be more interesting than he had thought.

He'd been all for the operation from the outset. He couldn't deny he had a thrill of excitement when he had first heard about it. It wasn't often intrasolar trips were made, and he'd been eager to experience a new environment, while enjoying the thrill of an actual live mission. And one for revenge at that.

He'd been a soldier in Varus' military for eight years now. Years of training and discipline. He'd seen his share of combat — skirmishes, putting down several insurgent groups on Varus, and the like. But this had been his first combat mission against Seutura. The first for anyone in decades, really.

He had hoped to have seen at least a little more resistance. He'd been itching for an excuse to put his training to use. But what he had seen tempered that. There hadn't been so much as an armed guard on the mining transport. And those who attempted to fight back seemed driven by mindless panic rather than any combat skill or desire to protect others.

Some of the other grab missions must have seen some action. He wished he'd been a part of one of those instead — like the one who had gone after the Seuturan military training center. The mine these workers worked at was a strategic target. There was a reason Varus had struck there.

He knew it should bother him that the girl was an innocent pawn in all this — and he had to admit he felt a twinge of guilt. But then, the Varus citizens who had died at Seuturan hands were innocent as well. Varus could have easily retaliated by wiping out some of their settlements, but upper command had decided to go with a more creative approach. No one was supposed to be seriously harmed this way — he grimaced thinking of the mishap in the hangar — but taking captives would still get the point across rather emphatically.

Ram leaned his head against the wall, closed his eyes, and let out a long sigh. The adrenaline was starting to wind down. Maybe the weight he had felt from the first reports of the Seuturan attack against Varus citizens would ease off him soon, now that he had done his part.

The hatch slid open, and he straightened. He found himself staring into the furious eyes of his captive.

"I am not wearing this!"

Ram quirked his head, wondering why she would say that. She had put it on, after all. The dark red dress fit her well. The chest had an elegant criss-cross pattern of wrapped cloth that led up to a wide, single shoulder enclosure. The skirt draped down elegantly to ankle-length, and had enough flow to allow for easy movement. It was a common Varusian fashion, though he had to admit he thought it looked better on her than anyone else he'd seen in similar styles.

She cleaned up nicely, he thought. Gone were the threadbare clothes, which were downright unsuitable for the mountains he'd taken her from. And it made him more than a little angry to think of her working in the cold, dank mines so poorly outfitted.

She'd pulled her long hair back into a single tie. And her crystal blue eyes were stunning, even when they were looking at him with such hostility.

He wondered if it was the dress that upset her, or the fashion of it.

"It's a dress," she said, clenching her fists. "And I'll freeze."

"It's a myth," he said, refraining from rolling his eyes.

"What?!"

"About how cold spaceships are," he explained. "Ours are well heated. In fact, keeping it cool enough is the real problem." It wasn't that difficult. The ship was insulated enough to keep the naturally generated heat from the equipment and people inside the ship. Thermal exchangers maintained the proper temperature, and shunted excess heat to be radiated off into space.

She looked at him as though he'd sprouted another head. He idly wondered if Seuturan ships didn't have proper insulation or other thermal equipment.

He stood. "It's time to go. Follow me." He put a little command in his voice, hoping he didn't have to carry her again. It was for her own safety that she needed to listen to him.

She bristled, and for a moment he thought she wouldn't come, but she stepped towards him, only favoring her cut foot slightly. He couldn't help but be amused by her attitude. She was compliant enough, but not cowering meekly. She was definitely going to be interesting.

"Why am I here?" she asked as they left the processing room. He couldn't miss the edge of fear in her voice that he could tell she was working hard to control. He felt the inexplicable urge to comfort her. Which was ridiculous, of course. He didn't want to terrify her, especially after the incident she'd seen in the hangar bay. But a little healthy fear might ensure she didn't do something reckless and get herself hurt.

As for why she was here…that would be an interesting conversation, wouldn't it? It was a topic he really didn't want to get into yet.

He needed to get her foot looked at and then he needed to get back to his squad. His squad leader, Thekla was already going to be ticked. He wasn't known for his patience and understanding on the best of days. The fact that Ram had *technically* disobeyed an order wasn't going to sit well. Ram was normally fairly well disciplined. Varus' military excelled because they were good at executing orders quickly and flawlessly. He'd need to go take the tongue-lashing meekly and promise to never do something so foolish again.

"I'll explain later," he told her. Poor woman had to be overwhelmed, and possibly in a mild state of shock. She had seen a fellow Seuturan citizen killed in front of her. He'd save the longer explanation for later.

It was just a short distance to the medbay. He kept an eye on her gait, trying to assess if her foot was hurt too badly. She favored it a little as they walked, but at this point it would be worse for him to pick her up again. Better she comply under her own volition.

The medbay had only a few people being treated as they walked in, including a few Seuturan prisoners. It wasn't busy yet. He was lucky he hadn't had to retrieve her from the holding pen. This place would be full by the time they were done. There had been a number of other injuries he'd seen as he passed by the captives. The Varus military self control had been strained under the events of the last few months, and any captives that had put up even the semblance of a fight got the brunt of it — such as the captive in the hangar bay.

Ram led the girl to the back of the medbay. He was surprised she had managed to run through a rocky, forest mountainside missing one boot. She was definitely favoring her good foot, but was trying not to. There were other possible injuries as well. He had tried to restrain her without hurting her, but she had struggled hard.

And she was bound to have some other health issues from working in the mines, in who knew what kind of hellish conditions. Hopefully nothing some good nutrition and a fusion injection wouldn't clear up.

He brought her over to one of the stations and gestured to the med bed. "Hop up, Buttercup. Going to have one of the medics look at your foot."

She glared at him, crossing her arms. "Why do you keep calling me that?"

"Your hair," he said, amused as he reached out to touch it. She jerked back. She was dealing with a lot, he chided himself.

"Hello, Corporal," a familiar voice said. The medic carried a small data pad in his hands as he stepped up beside them.

"Stefan!" Ram said with a grin. He gave the man a slap on the back. "Wondered if I'd bump into you here. How's it going so far?"

Stefan took the slap with a roll of his eyes and made his way over to bed. The man had a slight limp due to a genetic abnormality that affected the bones in his left leg. Ram had known Stefan for a number of years. They'd been stationed at the same military base in Varus' capital city of Khadako. Stefan had been declined for military service due to that limp, but he had still wanted to serve and so he'd become a medic — and a hell of a good one at that.

"I haven't seen anything that serious so far," Stefan said, "though I heard someone was brought to the secondary medbay for surgery. And I already heard about the incident in the hangar..." He glanced between Ram and his captive. "Sorry," he said apologetically to her. "The soldier will be disciplined for that. I know that isn't enough, but it will happen."

"That shouldn't have happened," Ram told her quietly. "What you saw in the hangar bay was…" Ram shook his head, jaw clenched. She just looked at him, and he wondered if she believed him.

"Would you tell me your name, please?" Stefan asked her.

"Carina Mosaido," his prisoner said.

"Any injuries?" Stefan asked, looking her up and down assessingly.

"Right foot," Ram said before she could speak up. "Anything else hurting, Buttercup?"

She scowled at him and shook her head.

"Right, well, Carina, please hop up and I'll get it looked at," Stefan said.

She — Carina — pushed herself up onto the med bed and Stefan leaned in to examine her foot.

"So you listen to him without protesting," Ram said teasingly.

Carina gave Ram an annoyed look. "He actually asked for my name, and used it. Politely."

Ram shrugged. The moment her cap had come off and he saw her hair, it reminded him of the flowers his mother had growing in their garden when he was younger. He didn't know why the endearment Buttercup had stuck in his head, but it had. He'd seen similar scowls from his sisters at the nicknames they'd ended up stuck with because of him. Though one had objected, albeit futilely, to Poppy, which he'd dubbed her after the time Ram had scared her with a toad as a child. She had bolted upright so fast that her hair flew up into the air, and both the motion and the resulting visual of her hair splayed out had reminded Ram of the flower. The thought of his sisters brought a pang, which he quickly shoved down. He needed to focus on getting his captive taken care of, and then get back to duty.

Ram frowned and leaned forward, eyeing Carina's right shoulder as Stefan began to clean and bandage her foot — the skin was scratched there as well. It looked like it was no longer bleeding, but it was irritated. She'd probably gotten it climbing through that window or on her attempted wild run through the forest.

"Stefan, make sure you look at her shoulder too, when you're done," Ram said, reaching to move her arm slightly to get a better look.

"Don't touch me!" She yanked her arm away.

Ram straightened up, looming over her. He hardened his expression as he looked down at her, letting his soldier training take over. Carina shrank back, eyes widening. It was time to establish some boundaries.

"Listen up. You are my responsibility right now. Your safety and well-being are my priority. There's no negotiating or cajoling, or whatever you think it is you're going to do to get me to do what you want. You'll do exactly as I say, understand?"

Her nose flared and he saw her jaw clench. She had enough spirit to not be completely cowed by his presence. But she was going to have to learn very quickly how things worked here, or this wasn't going to go well, for either of them.

Stefan cleared his throat. "I can take a look at that shoulder now."

Ram took a step back, raising an eyebrow at Carina. She turned to show her shoulder to Stephan, but continued glowering at Ram.

"I'd like a full blood workup and body scan as well," Ram added. Carina looked at him in disbelief, and it seemed like she was about to protest. He gave her a look. "You've worked in the mines for what...five, six years now? And you look as though you probably don't get enough to eat. You're having a full workup. It'll be my hide if you die of a preventable disease or malnutrition while in Varus custody."

She took a breath, and Ram could see she was seething. Before she could open her mouth, Stefan interrupted, "The blood draw will be quick and painless, and the scan will just take a moment. Now, I need you to lay back for me." Carina looked to Stefan, and Ram could see she was practically trembling, though whether from anger or just adrenaline from the entire situation he didn't know. Stefan smiled kindly at her. "I'm really just here to help. Nothing to worry about." She hesitated for a moment longer — long enough that Ram was tempted to snap at her to just lie down on the blasted bed. They really needed to get moving so he could get back to his squad.

Ram stood back, arms crossed. Stefan placed the blood draw device on her arm and then swabbed and bandaged her shoulder, all while the med scan ran. The scan was over and the blood was drawn before Stefan was finished with her shoulder. Carina looked with wonder at her arm as Stefan lifted the blood draw device off of it. There wasn't even the smallest mark.

Just how backward was their technology on Seutura?

"There's a small buildup in her left lung," Stefan said after the scan. "Nothing major, but there is some light scarring from microscopic irritants. But other than that and some vitamin deficiency, she's fine."

"I'll be fine," Carina said firmly, sitting up. Ram could tell that the idea of Varusian help for problems Seuturan technology couldn't fix rankled her.

"Yes, you will be," Stefan said, "once I give you this infusion."

Carina objected, but didn't try to bolt or escape, so Stefan was able to convince her to take the infusion without much protest. Ram tried to wait patiently. He didn't want to step on Stefan's toes, and he figured at this point butting in would just make things take longer, but Thekla was already going to have his hide. Ram needed to get his tail down to the squad room before he got in even bigger trouble than he was already in.

At last they were done, and Carina rose from the bed. Ram deposited the flat, black shoes on the floor, and she slipped them on. Then, with a quick farewell to Stefan, he ushered her past busy medics and other captives being treated and out of the medbay.

"Are you taking me to be with the other prisoners now?" she asked.

"No."

She froze in the middle of the hallway, jaw dropping open. "What? Why?"

Ram sighed and pushed her to the side of the walkway, nodding an apology to the crew members that had been walking behind them.

"I think it's past time for an explanation," she said, shoving his hands away and taking another step back.

Ram gave a small sigh. Time was ticking, he knew, but it wouldn't do to come in with a screaming captive in tow, which is what he suspected may happen if he just tossed her over his soldier and hurried to the squad. He just had to choose carefully what information he gave her.

She had already had to deal with a lot today, and he didn't want to add to that. So he'd give her what he felt he safely and in good conscience could. "Okay, here's the short version: you and your fellow Seuturans onboard this ship are currently prisoners of war, until negotiations with the Seutura government conclude and you are informed otherwise. A small portion of the prisoners, such as yourself, will be assigned under the care of Varusians and integrated into our crew. The bulk of the others will remain in holding facilities."

Carina was slack jawed at this point. "Are...are we going to be killed?" His chest tightened at the scared stutter he heard in her voice.

"No," he said, once again internally cursing that soldier in the hangar bay.

"But...a war?" she asked, her voice sounding weak. "There is no war."

"There is now," he said grimly, grabbing hold of her arm. He didn't have time for her to understand, and he sure wasn't going to walk away in hopes that she would follow. "Now I have places to be."

"Wait — but I don't understand..."

"Join the club, Buttercup."

Chapter 4

War. There was a war.

There had never been an all out war between Varus and Seutura — not as long as their history recorded at least. There'd been tension at times, even a small dispute or two over research station placement. But an *attack*? *War*? Never.

Carina stood beside Ram, staring blankly as he meticulously cleaned and stored each piece of his armor. She'd been in a daze since he'd told her. Now she just felt...numb.

They were in a long room with rows of armor storage lockers that seemed like they were coded to each soldier. Half-a-dozen other soldiers worked and chatted around them, doing similar tasks. She recognized a few from the flight. She was the only captive she could see in the room. A few gave her curious looks, but Ram mostly ignored them. For those who were too curious his glare was enough to turn their attention back to their tasks.

"One of the transports took some fire over Rimun," one of the nearby soldiers with an intricately inked tattoo on his right arm was telling another. "Got here okay, but will have to get transferred down to the maintenance bay."

"I heard we lost a pilot over Tarey in the northern hemisphere," the other soldier said grimly.

The first one let out a curse. "MIA or confirmed dead?"

"His fighter's transponder blew up when he was hit. An explosion that close to the cockpit could only mean one thing."

The two walked off, continuing their discussion about the results of the attack. Carina tried to listen but their voices grew indistinct before they said anything else of interest.

How could she not have at least heard a rumor about what was happening? She didn't even know exactly *what* had happened. Ram had been more somber since he'd told her, and quieter. She wanted to demand to know more, but something held her back.

There had been no hint of anything in the news casts. Nothing about the Varusians. And certainly nothing about any incidents or a war. She couldn't imagine that something like that would have been kept a secret. But it wasn't as though she followed the news much anyway, besides what she overheard during the trips up to the mines.

Her planet was at war. And if this ship was an indicator of their technology and weapons, Seutura was pitifully outmatched. If they had attacked the capital or any military installations, then the damage must be immense. What little defense and fighting force they had was likely crushed by the Varusians. Her chest tightened. She might not even have a home to go back to.

But then why capture all the prisoners? Was there a strategic purpose? Was it just retaliation? Perhaps the Varusians were taking them as slaves. Carina pulled her arms even tighter against herself.

"Ramnock!" The shout jolted her out of her stupor, and she jerked back toward Ram's storage locker.

A massive, angry man stood at the end of the row of lockers, still fully armored. He was bald, and a scar ran down the left side of his face, just grazing his eye. She wondered where he could have gotten such a scar, and also if she should be fleeing right now. But she remained frozen in place.

Ram set his next armor piece down in its spot with both haste and deliberate care. He stood up at attention with a neutral expression on his face. "Yes, sir?"

"What in the black void of space were you thinking?" the man roared, storming up to Ram. Carina pressed herself up against the weapon locker, eyes darting between the two men. Perhaps this *was* a good time to flee. If a fight broke out, she didn't want to be anywhere near the two of them — plus she might be able to get away in the resulting chaos. Not that she had anywhere to get away to.

"You're scaring my captive, sir," Ram said.

Scaring was an understatement. Carina was terrified. If she ever had imagined what a fierce, Varusian warrior looked like, this man in front of Ram would check every box.

Undaunted, the large man let out a growl. "You had orders." This must be Thekla, whom the other soldiers had been talking about. She had come to understand Ram shouldn't have chased her down. So why had he?

"I had to improvise," Ram stated matter-of-factly.

"Blast it, Ram, what do you think all the training and prep for the last year was?"

"So we got extra time to enjoy your pretty face, sir?" Ram asked. Carina's eyes went wide. Was he suicidal? He was trying to keep a straight face, but she could see the corners of his lips twitch.

But Thekla didn't seem to get any angrier than he already was. Finally he let out a long sigh. "You know Kasperi is going to have my hide for this, which means—"

"You gotta have mine, yeah, I know." Ram grinned.

"You're going to get an official reprimand from Admiral Untamo and command. They might not even let you keep the girl." Carina held her breath. Did that mean she would be put back with the other prisoners?

"That's not negotiable." Ram's face had gone deadly serious.

"That's not your decision." Thekla said firmly. He softened after a moment. "But I'll do my best. The final decision isn't mine either." Thekla glanced over at Carina, then back to Ram. "Hope she was worth it. Because training is going to be hell."

"For the week?"

"For the foreseeable future," he said as he turned to leave. Ram grimaced.

Carina felt hope flutter in her chest. If she was taken from him, perhaps she'd be moved back with the rest of her people. She'd still be a prisoner, but at least she'd have familiarity around her, and maybe a chance to find someone she knew. It wasn't that she hoped Bryn got captured too or anything, but it would be nice to see a familiar face.

But her hope was probably unfounded. Ram had said they were trying to split some of the prisoners among the crew. There was a chance she'd just be given to someone else. And Ram hadn't hurt her, at least — with the exception of twisting her wrist to make her drop the rock she had tried to hit him with. Being given to another random Varusian was a terrifying prospect. Better the devil she knew.

*   *   *

By the time they made their way to *Architeuthis'* main dining hall a couple hours later, for what Ram announced was dinner — apparently the ship time they held to was different than the time zone she lived in on Seutura — she felt exhausted.

They had spent quite a bit of time in the armor storage area. Ram had completed a number of tasks — mostly care for his armor and the gear he had carried into battle today — all while chatting merrily away with the other soldiers. She tried to remain inconspicuous, which seemed to work for the most part because the other soldiers ignored her.

Ram, however, did not. He was constantly making sure she was within his line of sight, occasionally handing her things — armor or tools — which she stood silently holding until he took them back. She considered each of them, wondering if any would be a useful weapon. But there was nothing remotely useful or small enough to hide. He would also grab her arm — though never too firmly — to move her around if she wasn't as fast as he wanted her to be. She debated resisting or even fighting back, but this didn't seem like the time. She didn't know whether it was wisdom or cowardice on her part. If she did try something, would she end up like that man in the hangar bay? Ram said it shouldn't have happened, but it *had*.

The constant stream of new people, stimulation, and situations left her barely hanging on by a thread. Her first sight of the massive mess hall that could host hundreds of crew members stretched that thread to its limit.

The hall wasn't full yet, but people were flowing in through the hatches around the room. The mess hall was enormous, with rows of dark gray tables and chairs lining the space. Ram led her down the steps from the hatch they had entered at the upper level balcony that ran part way around the edge of the room. Decorative lighting hung down in curved loops that swooped toward the tables. She spotted a few women in similar dress as her, and some men with what looked like the male version of it. They were scattered, almost lost amidst all the Varusians. The tables had a portion down the middle that jutted upward, and she saw people reaching in and pulling out metal trays of food.

Ram led her, weaving through the crowds of people. All of the Varusians seemed in good spirits as laughter rang out, and animated conversations went on all around them. She tensed as she felt the unfamiliar crowd pressing in around her, the din of loud voices overwhelming her.

Finally Ram stopped at a table near one curved corner of the room, but not quite at the edge. He guided her to sit in one of the chairs beside another man. He looked like a soldier as well, with close cropped hair and the standard casual uniform as Ram.

"Ram!" he said brightly. He raised his eyebrows as he saw Carina, and looked back at Ram who slid into the chair next to her. "Hey there," he said. "I'm Kovar."

"Carina," she said, taking his hand after a moment of hesitation.

"Nice to meet you," Kovar said. "Though I'm sorry your introduction to us had to be through Ram." Ram snorted as he began pulling trays out of the center console. "He treating you okay?"

"Um, yes?" Carina said, unsure how she should answer that question and why he was being so friendly with her. She had expected animosity or ambivalence. Her eyes dropped down to the tray and cup Ram had placed in front of her. Some of it looked familiar — a vegetable she knew she had seen at one point, and some bread. But she was surprised to see such a large serving of meat. She glanced at Ram's tray. It held similar items, though he had a much larger portion.

"Just let me know if you need more," Ram said, nodding toward her plate. He began devouring the food in front of him.

Carina began hesitantly — unable to resist taking a bite of the meat. They rarely got meat on Seutura. They were only able to breed a small number of animals for food — they just didn't thrive well in the harsh environment. So it was a rare delicacy indeed. They usually had protein-based paste, developed from a root plant that managed to grow decently well on her planet.

As it hit her tongue, she realized she had never tasted anything like it. This was tender and had seasoning she couldn't place. She couldn't believe they not only had access to so much meat, but were able to preserve and transport it so well. She idly wondered if they had live animals on board. And the seasoning — perhaps they were able to grow plants far better on Varus.

"Why don't you have captives?" Carina asked the soldiers around her, uncertain if she should speak up at all.

"Ah, not all of us are as lucky as Ram," Kovar said with a grin. "Heard you smashed open a window and helped someone else out before saving yourself. Impressive. No wonder Ram fudged orders a bit to go grab you."

Lucky me, Carina thought with irritation.

"Only a small number of captives are being integrated into the crew, for security reasons," Ram explained, ignoring Kovar's teasing to actually answer her question. "The rest will remain in the holding areas."

She stiffened as Ram casually rested his arm behind on the low backrest of her chair, but he didn't seem to notice as he continued his conversation with Kovar.

"Any word on our missing soldiers?"

"Not much good," Kovar replied grimly. "We did get a distress call from one. A rescue unit went in and was able to get him out. Got a little banged up on the way out, but they're on an intercept course with us." He took a sip from the cup in front of him. "No word on our pilot that went down near Tarey. No working transponder and no way of knowing if he even survived. They're assuming casualty at this point."

Ram cursed softly. "Any retaliation?"

"Nothing significant. We're in a stable, safe upper orbit. Just waiting for the higher-ups to commence with negotiations." Kovar looked as though he was going to say something else, but he looked at Carina and hesitated. Something unspoken seemed to pass between the two soldiers, and they changed subjects to something mundane.

Carina felt herself relax a fraction. Upper orbit. That meant they still had to be close to Seutura. And if negotiations were happening soon, there was hope. Varus hadn't just wiped out Seutura. Her government would get this all sorted out. She would go home, eventually. She just had to survive until then.

The conversation droned on around her but it became just a muted, buzzing sound, as Carina stared listlessly at her plate. She had eaten a decent amount — it was delicious, and she wanted to keep her strength up. But her thoughts were a thousand kilometers from here. She really just wanted to be home — to be eating in her tiny kitchen, with her herb plants, curling up in her own cot. She wanted to run errands tomorrow and then to go back to work in a couple days with Bryn and her other co-workers.

She wanted to be where it was familiar. Where it was safe.

Instead, she was in an enemy spaceship, far away from her home and everything she knew. And she was under the care of an imposing man, with no idea what his intentions were. The half-picked-at meal in front of her blurred.

She nearly fell out of the chair when a strong hand firmly gripped her arm. "Time to go, Buttercup."

Chapter 5

"I'm not going to hurt you." Ram's words startled her as he led her through the corridors.

She looked warily over at him, unsure how to even respond to that. Besides taking her to begin with, he hadn't been cruel. But the day wasn't over yet.

Not hurt her. She didn't know what that even meant. What being a *captive* really meant. Why had he taken special notice of her? To bring her back to his bed? She could fight — she *would* fight. But he was so much bigger and a trained soldier. She had little hope of fending him off.

"I mean, I'm not going to...take advantage of you." His words were halting, almost awkward, and it was the most flustered she'd seen him so far.

"Right." She wished she could believe him, but she wasn't naive. She was an enemy captive.

The room Ram took her to was basically cube shaped, and held a couch with plush, dark-blue cushions in front of a low table made of some glossy black material that had a metallic rim running around the edge. There was a large viewscreen recessed into one wall, currently displaying an expanse of stars. Several cabinets built into other walls, and a tall table with several chairs around it was in one corner.

All in all, it wasn't large, but even with the various furniture it managed to not feel cramped. On each side of the room she noticed a door, more like a hatch than anything. One was open and she noticed the corner of what looked like a very comfortable bed.

These are his quarters, she realized. *He took me back to his quarters.*

The thought jolted Carina, bringing the wave of fear back to the forefront of her mind. She couldn't stop her trembling. He'd said he wouldn't take advantage of her, but he'd brought *here.*

And there was little she could use as a weapon. The chairs were sturdy but they looked heavy enough to be unwieldy, and there weren't many loose objects — a blanket strewn across the back of the couch, a datapad resting on a shield inlaid in the wall alongside a few other personal effects. Nothing she could hope would help.

His hand came up, brushed her arm, and she jerked away, colliding with the couch. She pressed herself up against the wall, breaths coming in rapid pants, watching him. "Don't touch me."

Ram looked at her quizzically. "Okay, Buttercup. Calm down."

"Calm down?" She laughed, and it sounded near hysterical to her ears. "How in the stars do you think I'll be calm right now? I've been stolen from everything I know by a barbarian who is going to ..." She gestured vaguely toward his bed.

"Whoa, hold on now!" Ram interrupted, holding up his hands, eyes growing wide. "I *told* you I'm not going to—"

"Do you think I'm stupid?" Carina snapped. "You took me back to your personal quarters!" What kind of game was he trying to play with her?

"I'm not going to take advantage of you," Ram said. "You're under my protection."

"As a *captive!*"

Ram growled, and Carina flinched back, bumping into the wall as Ram came close. But he simply brushed by her, going to the other hatchway and pressing the keypad on the side. The hatch slid open with a hiss. Ram gestured at it, scowling.

Carina inched along the wall, hands pressed behind her against the cool metal.

Inside was a small bed and side table, several cabinets built into the walls, and another open hatch which led into what looked like a tiny bathroom.

"Your room," Ram said.

She turned to look back at him, confused. He just stared at her, arms crossed. Curiosity got the better of her and she stepped inside, looking around.

"But—" she began.

"Are you unhappy with the arrangement?" Ram asked, raising his eyebrows.

She shook her head quickly.

"Good," he practically growled. "Breakfast is at seven. Be ready."

Before she could protest, or ask how she was supposed to tell what time it was, he slapped the keypad, the door slid closed.

She stood there for a moment in silence, her mind reeling and her hands still shaking. She'd been so sure, despite his words, he might force her, even hurt her. She'd been ready to fight. And then he surprised her. His anger was at what she had presumed about him and his intentions, that she hadn't believed his words. But wasn't that what barbarian victors did?

A part of her wondered if it was just a ploy — that he was just toying with her. But his anger had seemed so genuine that she wasn't sure. Still, she looked over the keypad from her side of the hatch, but she didn't see a way she could lock it.

She began to cautiously explore the room. The bed had crisp, comfortable bedding, with an extra soft blanket folded neatly at the end. The table beside the bed had the time, and what she assumed was a date in a format she didn't recognize, displayed on its surface. At least she'd know when she would need to be prepared to face Ram again.

An examination of the cabinets revealed neat rows of clothing and shoes in an array of beautiful colors and slight variations of the style she currently wore. There was a cushioned chair with a metal frame in the corner. It took some maneuvering, since it was heavier than it appeared, but she managed to move it in front of the hatchway. It wouldn't do much to slow him down if he tried to come in during the night, but it would give her some warning.

She couldn't stop trembling, and she had to force herself to take even breaths. She was safe, for now. She just had to convince her body of that.

Her brain could finally catch up on the last few minutes. Ram puzzled her. Everything she'd heard, even seen in the violence in the hangar bay, of Varusians led her to believe that of course he would just take what he wanted from her, but Ram didn't fit that picture. Even as an enemy captive, it seemed she had some safety. Perhaps this barbarian had lines even he wouldn't cross.

Now that she had a moment to be alone, to think, the weight of all that had happened that day pressed in on her. She missed Bryn. Carina could remember making mud pies together with Bryn at the small colony childcare center that they stayed with while their parents worked when they were just four years old. Carina had carefully made sets of mudpies on the rocks, while Bryn had thrown hers at the boys. They'd become instant friends.

Bryn would know exactly what to say and how to handle this whole mess. She'd probably have half the soldiers wound around her finger, and ticked the other half off in the same process.

Carina thought back to the conversation she and Bryn had been having on the transport just this morning, before this whole nightmare had begun.

"You doing anything fun for your free day?" Bryn asked.

Carina shrugged. "Normal errands and things. Going to see if I can get some more flour. Tennel offered to make a quick trip up with me to Wharton."

Bryn raised her eyebrows. "Hmm."

"And what are you hmming about?"

"He's certainly made his interest clear."

They kept their conversation low, though with the clamor of the clanking transport conversation could hardly be heard beyond the next person anyway.

Carina shrugged. "He's nice. And we'd get an extra quota of credits and a chance at nicer housing."

"How romantic," Bryn said, putting her hand to her forehead. "You know the only reason he's even interested in you is because you made him a loaf of your rosemary bread."

Carina let out a short laugh, and shook her head. "There are worse reasons. It's just practical, and we both know it. Neither of us are approaching it with any illusions." Carina gave Bryn a look. "As nice an idea of 'falling in love' is, it's not like we have many opportunities here."

"I know, I know," Bryn said, holding up her hands. "And I'm not saying to have your heads up in the clouds or anything. But you don't have to get married to the first guy that shows a modicum of interest."

Carina shrugged. Tennel was steady, dependable, and predictable. Honestly, that is all she wanted. Romantic notions were all well and good — she knew some people who got together and married for love — but it seemed, in her experience, those who got together for practical reasons seemed to do better.

And it wasn't that they were incompatible. She and Tennel got along well enough. He was neat and tidy, and didn't overindulge at the colony tavern. And Bryn was probably right — he did seem like her cooking. But that was fine by her.

"I could do a lot worse," she said

"And it's okay to have a little hope for the future. Far more than being a mindless, Seuturan drone."

"I do! I'm going to get married, get a better quota and housing. We both hope to put in a transfer request to an agriculture district, which will be a better place to raise a family."

Bryn shook her head. "That sounds a lot like surviving — not living."

Carina gave her a look. "Now who's the optimist?" They both broke into a laugh. Carina sobered, then shook her head with a small smile. "I'm content. I don't need miracles."

She hadn't thought about Tennel since this whole ordeal started. She didn't know what that said about her and him. He wasn't someone she loved. He was reliable. Predictable. She could use some of that right now.

Hopelessness and weariness washed over her as she looked about her room. Her prison quarters. She readied for bed, and finally, exhaustion overtaking every part of her body and mind, she curled up beneath the covers. Reliable and predictable were nice, but what Carina would give for a miracle right now.

*   *   *

Loud banging awoke her and she jerked upright, clutching the blanket to her as her heart threatened to burst out of her chest. Amazingly, she had slept well. Exhaustion from the events of the day before, combined with how comfortable the bed was, had won out over any lingering fears she might have felt.

"Fifteen minutes, Buttercup. Don't keep me waiting," Ram's voice called loudly from outside the metal door to her room.

She slowly let out a breath as she heard his footsteps stomp away.

She didn't waste any time. She dressed quickly in a dark blue dress with short sleeves and an intricately woven top that flowed down into a long skirt. She had slept in her braid, and a lot of it had come loose in the night. She let it all down, and hastily pinned it back with some pins she found in the cabinet in the bathroom.

Carina was trying to move the heavy chair away from the hatchway when she heard footsteps approach, and several loud pounds on the door. "Time's up, Buttercup."

"Just a second!" she called out, giving the chair another shove.

The hatchway slid open with a hiss, and she jerked her head up, meeting the green eyes and scowling face of her captor. He was already dressed in his uniform. He looked sharp — far too good looking for this early in the morning. And it annoyed her that she was even thinking that way about an enemy soldier.

"What in the stars are you doing?" Ram asked, looking between her and the chair.

"There's...uh, no lock. On the door," she said, blushing, and feeling angry at herself for doing so. It was his own blasted fault she felt like she needed to defend herself as best as she could. She shouldn't be embarrassed about it.

Ram let out a curse about stars and things that couldn't possibly happen to them in reality. He waved her away from the chair. She stepped back, crossing her arms. He put a booted foot on the edge of the chair, and gave it a shove. It slid and hit the wall with a dull thud.

"Let's go," he said, turning to leave. Carina sighed and trudged out behind him.

Ram remained grouchy all through breakfast, hardly speaking to her. She didn't know what was with him this morning. He seemed far more surly than he had been the day before. She didn't want to provoke him, so she kept quiet throughout the meal and hoped she'd have a chance to glean anything helpful later. She just felt a small bit of relief, edged with caution. Things weren't quite as bad as she'd first thought. Ram hadn't hurt her. Negotiations were supposed to start soon. Maybe that's something else that would go better than she had feared.

She had hoped he would sit next to someone he knew — or better yet, next to another Seuturan captive — and that she'd have a chance to overhear any new information. But the dining hall was much emptier than the night before, and they sat by themselves.

She did her best to enjoy breakfast. There was some kind of mashed grains, topped with fruit she didn't recognize and a sprinkle of what looked like sugar. And there was even meat sausages on the side. She savored each bite, though she tried not to take too long when she saw how quickly Ram was scarfing down breakfast.

She observed the mess hall while she ate. It seemed like the color of uniforms delineated different types of crew members. Soldiers, like Ram, wore black. The medic who had cared for her yesterday had worn a light shade of blue. She saw some gray and brown sprinkled throughout those eating breakfast in the dining hall, but she couldn't quite figure out what they meant.

She almost broke her resolve to remain quiet after breakfast when he led her through the ship. Down lifts, through corridors, and a couple sets of steps. She still had no idea how anyone managed to find their way through this maze of a ship without so much as glancing at a map. They finally reached a large room with a dome ceiling that glowed in a way that reminded her of sunlight. Sections of the floor were broken apart in large hexagonal shapes, roughly ten meters across, each colored differently. The floor itself was peculiar. As soon as her feet touched it, they sank in ever so slightly. It was made from some type of padded material. And she quickly saw why.

There were a few groups of men fighting within the marked off sections of flooring. It took her a moment to realize they were just practicing, and there was no real aggression in their moves. In one group she saw a man grapple with and throw his partner, but when he hit the floor, he wasn't seriously injured as far as she could tell. The floor seemed to absorb the brunt of the impact.

Ram led her over to an alcove that was still a part of the larger room, but had a glass wall partially blocking it from the main area. He grabbed something from a nearby cabinet and passed it to her. She took the strange, flexible flask.

"Drink," he said. Then he gestured to the padded bench. "Sit."

Before Carina could snap at him that she wasn't a dog, he had already stalked away toward a group of men in one of the colored areas of the room. She scowled and slammed the flask down on the bench beside her. Infernal barbarian.

Chapter 6

Ram slammed Feingo onto the padded ground for a third time. Feingo let out a wheezing curse. Ram tried to feel satisfied he'd taken him down. But there was still a restless, anger-fueled energy that seemed to fill him.

"You alright?" Feingo asked as Ram offered him a hand up.

Ram grunted. "Ready to go again?"

"No, I need a minute," Feingo said, shaking his head. "You need to cool off?"

Cool off? No, he needed to burn through it. Push until the anger faded away at least a little.

"Seeing action made you a wimp?" Ram asked, rolling his left shoulder. It was still a little sore from where he'd hit the ground yesterday chasing after Carina. He should have it looked at. While he wanted to brush it off as nothing, if it *was* more than a bit of soreness, he wanted to make sure it was taken care of. He'd known more than one soldier who'd ignored injuries and later regretted it when the damage had become permanent and they were deemed no longer fit for service.

Feingo ignored the jab and gave him an assessing look. "Girl giving you trouble?"

Ram laughed. "Does she look like she can give me trouble?" Feingo glanced over at her, and Ram had the inexplicable urge to put a fist in his face.

Feingo reached down and grabbed a towel, then turned to move off their section of the training room. Ram growled out, "She thought I was going to take advantage of her." Ram had been shocked by her assumption last night, after he had tried to explain. She hadn't believed his assurances.

That was compounded by seeing the violence in the hangar bay by an undisciplined soldier and by the news that he'd received later last night that one of the captive women *had* been harmed by a group of men. It had sparked a fury in him that he'd thought he'd put to rest months ago.

Varus society was far from perfect. There was war and brutality throughout their history. It was better now than it had been — and having their leader, Imperator Mallakis, begin enforcing stricter guidelines had gone a long way toward protecting women and changing how their social customs worked. But change was often slow — much slower than he thought was right for a society as advanced as theirs. And as hard as the Imperator pushed, he was facing a wall of deep-seated culture and people with power who were less inclined to be civilized. When some of those in upper command and the bureaucracy were still ingrained in the old ways and protected those who acted unscrupulously, it made change even harder.

He was grateful Thekla was strict with his squad, and for the bond they shared together. Ram would trust any of them with his life, or Carina's if it came down to it. But, as last night's attack on the Seuturan woman showed, corruption was pervasive. From what he heard, there were going to be consequences, but some of the high-ups were still pushing against it. He hoped justice would win out and the consequences would be swift and brutal.

Every time he thought about the incident, he pictured Carina's face as the victim. He wouldn't let that happen. That's why today he planned to always keep her in sight. But the idea that it could have been her...his jaw clenched up at the thought.

Feingo stopped, and turned back toward him, wiping off his forehead with his towel. "What made her think that?" Feingo asked. Ram shrugged. "Did you, you know, explain things to her?"

"Yeah, of course."

Feingo gave him a look. "Like, *really* explained?"

Ram shifted slightly. "Might have left out a few details. But she was already dealing with a lot of new information — I didn't want to overwhelm her." And there were certainly things Ram didn't want to get into at all. "Didn't think she'd jump to crazy conclusions."

Feingo snorted. "What did you expect? It's not like Seuturans have a favorable view of us to begin with. You add that to the mix of taking a girl back to your quarters—"

"I was taking her back to her room! I told her I wouldn't take advantage of her. And it's how all the integrated captives are set up."

"And you informed her all about that ahead of time?" Fengo asked, crossing his arms. "What's she going to think when she just arrives at your quarters?"

Ram growled. "I don't take advantage of women."

"Right. But you think she magically knows that? You're going to have to be clear with her to earn her trust, and it's going to take time. Communication, man. Communication." Feingo shook his head.

"She's a captive. She should do as she's told, and not jump to foolish conclusions." Ram hadn't anticipated having a captive would be much trouble at all. When he had signed up for the opportunity, it had just been another faceless Seuturan in his mind. It was supposed to be straightforward and easy. He would have someone help out with his duties, and he'd enjoy bossing someone around as the face of the people who had caused Varus trouble. And he'd also be fulfilling a personal duty and vow.

It had taken some finagling on the comms with someone from upper command last night to sort out the whole situation. Technically, the hostages to be integrated were to be distributed by request first, and then by lottery, up to a certain limit so they wouldn't compromise the security of the ship. However, there had been more requests beforehand than the allotted limit for the ship, so he was supposed to have put in another request after the hostages were processed. He'd received an earful for taking Carina through processing without full authorization. He'd meekly accepted the verbal chastening, but thanks to his excellent record — and what he was sure must have been some string-pulling by Thekla, and likely his superior Commander Halvar — he'd been given full authorization to care for Carina.

She hadn't really been trouble. But she had been perplexing. It had caught him off guard last night — hadn't even crossed his mind that she wouldn't believe him. When he'd first grabbed her, he'd felt indifferent to her fear — even a little glad, if he was being honest. After all, wasn't it what Seuturans deserved? It mattered little to him that she personally hadn't been a part of what had transpired to start this war in the first place. The hostages had been taken for a purpose. Varus had to send a clear message. She was a bargaining chip.

But seeing her fear in his quarters last night — that had cut him deeper than he knew how to deal with right now. He hadn't expected it to draw up such strong emotions in him.

Feingo let out a laugh. "I don't know that you fully thought this through."

"You two done gabbing and ready to get some real work in?" Thekla called from across the area.

"Yes, sir," they called out. Feingo chuckled as they made their way to the rest of the group.

Chapter 7

"The armguards go here," Ram was explaining as he showed Carina exactly how the armor pieces fit into his locker unit. They had just spent the last hour scrubbing all the parts of the armor with a mixture that smelled rather foul to her, but apparently helped keep the armor in good repair. He had repeatedly corrected her scrubbing technique, until she'd been nearly ready to dump the cleaning mixture over his head.

She saw again the intricate designs carved on the armor pieces as she handled most of Ram's armor today. They were etched into the very material itself with some technique that left very fine and precise lines and shapes. A quick glance around the other squad member's armor told her they were definitely unique designs. On Ram's she noticed several creatures and a few etchings that were clearly symbolic, but most of them left her clueless as to their meaning. In the upper left of the chest piece, blending into the other etchings, one caught her eye. It was clearly in a prominent place, even if difficult to make out at first glance. It depicted a woman holding a small child. Her fingers automatically traced over it.

She didn't mind the work itself. This was mild compared to the labor she normally did. She was used to work that put calluses on her hands and never-ending stiffness in her muscles. The first couple hours had been just sitting while the soldiers sparred and did various training exercises. Ram kept looking over at her throughout the session. It made her feel nervous. His looks never felt lascivious, but she grew annoyed as he kept it up. Was he afraid she would try to run away here in the midst of all these soldiers? After a couple hours of that, it felt good to be doing something with her hands.

She was amazed at the dedication the Varusians had toward training. Their motions were clean and smooth. She had seen the squad do the same motions in a drill over and over again with the same precision the last time as the first. She wondered how long they'd been preparing for this attack to demonstrate such a high level of skill.

Seutura had a military of sorts, but nothing to this extent. It was mostly to guard restricted areas and essential services, and quell the occasional uprising. But from what she'd seen and heard, their numbers were small and they primarily relied on their weaponry to do what they needed to do. She was surprised by the extent to which she saw the Varusian soldiers practice hand-to-hand combat. Other than a few practice blades, she saw no other weapons during the training time. They clearly had at least marginally superior technology than even the most advanced she'd seen on Seutura. It was curious to her that they didn't use it. Or perhaps it was that they just didn't rely on it.

When he first gave her the task of cleaning his armor, Ram had explained that all the crew members had different duties, and all of the soldiers chipped in to help with various other tasks on board with a rotating schedule. Ram said the soldiers usually trained in the morning, and they had an assigned task for the afternoon — cleaning, maintenance, and whatever else needed to be done on board. That had surprised her as well. She would have thought the military personnel were above the regular tasks of other crew members. She tried to imagine Ram or any of the other trained soldiers dealing with garbage, and it just seemed strange to her.

When they finally finished and stored the last armor piece, Ram rose to his feet, gesturing for her to follow.

He led her out of the room. It was too early for lunch — at least she thought so, but her body was still adjusting to the ship's time. Ram seemed like he was in a better mood than earlier that morning — perhaps beating on his squad mates and working up a sweat had released some tension. So she decided to dare ask a question.

"Where are we going?"

He hesitated for a long moment, not pausing his steps, but he did look at her curiously. Then shook his head, and grinned. "You'll see."

Carina scowled, feeling irritation well up again. And she couldn't decide if the grin was a good sign or not. But at least he hadn't bittern her head off just for asking a question.

She wondered if negotiations had started yet. She hoped so. She had to admit she wasn't sure how much the Seutura government valued their citizens' individual lives, but they at least had to care that a portion of their workforce had disappeared. She was tempted to ask, but even with Ram's good mood she felt like this wasn't the time.

She had no idea what Varus would ask in return, though. It wasn't as though Seutura was resource-rich to begin with. And if Varus had wanted resources, why not just steal those instead of people? What could they possibly want that Seutura had?

She just hoped the negotiations would go quickly. She wanted to be back home. She wondered if Tennel was concerned about her. They had been talking about a very practical arrangement, but surely he had a small amount of concern about her safety.

Carina's reverie was cut short as Ram stopped them in front of a set of large doors. He keyed them open, then gestured for her to go inside. She did so — and instantly felt uneasy.

The room was very dark — lit only by a dim blue light from above. She couldn't make anything else out in the small, rectangular room. She drew back and collided into Ram's hard torso. He chuckled, and she felt it reverberate through his muscular chest before she jerked away.

"Scared of the dark, Buttercup? Thought you'd be comfortable with it — working in the mines."

The door slid shut behind them, plunging the room into even deeper darkness.

"Of course I'm not scared of the dark," she said, trying to keep her voice even as she eased away from where she could see his silhouette. She took a deep breath. He wouldn't take her somewhere unknown to take advantage of her, would he? Why here and not his room last night? She felt mostly confident in that, but still uneasy. "But there are no monsters in the dark of the mines."

"Ouch." She saw his silhouette advance toward her, and she retreated until her back hit the far side of the room. Still he prowled forward. "There are far more dangerous monsters in the galaxy you should watch for other than me."

"I'm more worried about the monster nearby than one in the distant part of the galaxy." She felt the heat from his body as he neared her, smelled him — clove and citrus mixed with the sweat that still clung to him from the exercises this morning. It was more pleasant than she cared to admit.

She debated making a dash for it — to one side or the other — but in the dark she couldn't see where the door was. There was nowhere she could go where he couldn't just catch her easily. All she could do was press herself against the cool metal behind her.

"Careful, Buttercup," he said softly, and she could just see the glint of his eyes in the dimness.

She was about to scoff at him, when the wall moved away from behind her. His arm caught her before she could fall, and he chuckled softly. She huffed in annoyance, and shoved. Her shove didn't affect him, but instead pushed her through the door that had just opened. Away from him.

And into the stars.

It took her a moment to orient herself. For a moment she felt like she was floating, but her feet were firmly on the ground. The room was almost as dark as the last one. Only the faintest glow that ran along a slim border right at the bottom edges of the pitch-black massive floor gave any artificial light. There were no walls. The door she had come through was the only opaque object. The rest of the room was just a glass dome that was nearly invisible, curving up over them. And the stars…

They were so bright — so crisp. Even on the clearest night up at the mountain colony, they'd never come close to looking like *this*. Like she could just reach out and run her hands through them, like sparkling grains of sand. She always knew the atmosphere distorted the light of the stars and made them twinkle, but she had never seen a picture of them from space. It was breathtaking.

Some sections were slightly cloudy compared to others, and for the first moments in her entire life, she felt the faintest longing to know what was beyond them.

She felt more than heard Ram come up beside her.

"It's—" she started to say softly. But couldn't find the words to complete what she wanted to say. Words seemed inadequate.

Ram was silent for a long moment. "Best place in the whole of *Architeuthis*," he said quietly. "Surprised it's not more crowded this morning."

She belatedly realized that there was a smattering of other people in the room — standing or relaxing in reclined seats that were spread throughout the space — silent or speaking in hushed tones, as if everyone could feel the reverence of the universe.

They stayed there for a long time, quietly watching the slowly rotating expanse of stars. And Carina wondered if this was Ram's way of apologizing — for her terror last night, for her capture, for the circumstances they've found themselves in. Not that it was enough. She didn't know if she could ever forgive the man who had taken her from everything she knew. But she would still savor the peace the stars brought.

Chapter 8

The calm state she'd managed to get herself into at the observatory lasted barely into the afternoon. After lunch, Ram informed her they were on cleanup duty in the main landing bay. He'd told her to change out of her dress and into a sort of jumpsuit he gave her. It was clearly meant to delineate her as a captive — the color was deep red, and it had a woven belt that cinched at the waist. Despite being a work jumpsuit, it still had decorative flourishes to it — a gold thread pattern stitched along the sides and upper arms.

Carina wasn't sure what to expect, and came along uneasily as Ram led her through the ship. She had no idea how he kept track of where to go. All of *Architeuthis* seemed like a giant maze to her. Every corridor and lift looked nearly identical to her — strange and foreign compared to what she knew. Though at one point the mines on Seutura had been like a maze to her as well, but now she could navigate those blindfolded. It had become a necessary skill as often the lights would cut out and leave areas in near darkness.

They passed several sets of heavily armed soldiers, some of whom greeted Ram. She kept her head mostly down, trying to stay close to Ram, but not too close.

As they reached their destination, she realized it was the same bay they had arrived in. It still looked mind-bogglingly huge to her. More than two dozen shuttles were spread out over the bay. They looked tiny with all the open space between them. Several other shuttles were being moved off into storage areas in the wings of the bay. The shuttles that remained in the bay each had a flurry of activity surrounding them.

Ram led her over to an area that was bustling with people. Groups of crew members were going in and out of shuttles throughout the bay. Through the open cargo bay of the shuttles, she could see several men dismantling the containment cages the Seutura's had been brought in. She averted her gaze as she saw someone using an air-pressure washer to clean off what looked like blood on a shuttle's ramp, a wave of nausea coming over her. Ram steered her away from there, toward one of the other transport ships.

She had the fleeting, insane thought that perhaps she could just run aboard and try to fly away in one. It was absurd given all the commotion going on. Not only were there crews working everywhere, but there were soldiers posted throughout the bay. She spotted a few standing inside the ships themselves. Even if by some miracle she could get away from Ram and get aboard one of the ships, she'd have to get past the crews and armed soldiers. She shuddered, remembering the captive who had been killed for resisting when they first arrived onboard.

And if she made it past the soldiers and crew alive, then what? It wasn't as though she had the first clue how to fly a transport. She'd likely end up crashing into something in the process. No, she wasn't going to do anything so suicidal.

Ram stopped them beneath the base of one of the transport ships. "Start rolling these up," he told her, gesturing at long, black mats that lay on the hangar floor.

Then he moved off to the side, speaking with another crew member who wore a gray jumpsuit as he began grabbing large, metal poles that were piled on the ground. Carina hesitated only a moment, then crouched down. Physical labor she could handle. The material was surprisingly flexible and lightweight, but seemed very durable. They rolled easily into tight bundles with little effort.

She kept an eye on Ram while she worked. He was carrying the poles to a nearby cart. As he moved farther away, the thought of running came to mind again. It was still foolish, but she couldn't help daydreaming about it. There were crew members and soldiers everywhere, and she stuck out like a sore thumb in her red jumpsuit. There were only a few others with red jumpsuits in the hangar — the nearest over fifty meters away. No hope of even getting help from one of them. She clenched her jaw and kept working. Better to bide her time and observe. The more docile she was, perhaps the more Ram would let his guard down. Hopefully at some point an opportunity would present itself. And she would be ready, she promised herself.

"Why, hello there," a voice from above her said. She tucked her head further down, continuing to work, keeping the mat taut so it remained tight as she rolled it. "Didn't know we'd manage to nab such a beautiful little captive."

Carina gritted her teeth, and kept working. The tone of the voice held a sinister playfulness to it. She didn't dare look up and invite more interaction. All she could do was pray that Ram was close by and that he truly didn't want anything bad to happen to her. She almost laughed at the irony — she'd been so annoyed by his constant presence, and now she was desperate for it.

"What's your name, love?" the voice said again, and a pair of boots came into view, stepping up onto the mat she was attempting to roll and blatantly blocking her path.

"I'm trying to work," she said, trying to sound meek but firm, while keeping her head down. Where was her stupid barbarian captor when she needed him?

"Just trying to have a friendly conversation." She froze as a hand came down and touched her chin, raising her head up. She repressed a shudder at the touch, but didn't dare pull back. The man was dressed in a white, fitted uniform, and the blue eyes that stared down at her were ones to be feared. He was clearly an officer, and Carina's hope that Ram would save her shrank. Could he save her from a superior? Ram hadn't said that *no one* would take advantage of her, only that he wouldn't. Would an officer of the Varusian military be more ruthless than its soldiers?

"Get your blasted hands off my captive, Mikael," came Ram's voice from behind her, full of vehemence.

She took advantage of the interruption and pulled away from the officer. Turning, she saw Ram's face. It was harder than she had ever seen it. Carina felt a swell of emotions wash over her. Anger that Ram had taken even this long. Surprise that he would talk that way to someone who was clearly an officer. And relief that the hand was no longer touching her chin.

"Oh, she's yours?" The man regarded her with a smile. She shivered — it was anything but friendly.

"Go jump out an airlock," Ram said.

Mikael just chuckled. "Is that any way to speak to a superior officer?" The tone implied just how superior an officer he was. He was the first one Carina had seen dressed in white. It must mean upper command. Carina tensed. She had already seen that Ram couldn't keep his mouth shut sometimes. He might land both of them in hot water. As terrified as Ram had made her yesterday, the feeling that overcame her when Mikael smiled at her was a thousand times worse.

"It is if he's putting his hands where he shouldn't be," Ram calmly replied. His face was still stony hard, and he seemed barely containing some kind of anger.

The man in white cocked his head. "Perhaps command was too hasty in granting your request. I ought to see if they'll...reconsider."

Ram snorted, coming up beside Carina. She stayed crouched on the floor, not wanting to draw any more attention to herself. She knew a power play when she saw one, and she wasn't about to get in the middle of it. "Not gonna happen, Mikael. Go find someone else to bother."

Mikael smirked, and with one last glance at Carina, walked away toward a group of men working with equipment beside another ship.

Ram crouched down next to her. "Sorry about that, Buttercup." He eyed her. "You good?"

"Fine." Her eyes flicked to the white uniformed man walking away from them. "Friend of yours?"

"Something like that. Every crew has their bad apples. I'll make sure he doesn't bother you again." He rose, stood over her a moment as if to reassure her with his presence, and then went back to moving equipment.

Carina returned to rolling up the mats, trying to ignore the shaking in her hands. It was a good reminder that she wasn't safe here. As kind as Ram had been to her, there were plenty of monsters among his people, like this officer and others who were out for blood. And though Ram had tried to assure her Mikael wouldn't bother her, she didn't put much faith in that. What could Ram do to protect her from a superior officer? Eventually Mikael could find an excuse to order her and Ram apart.

She wished she had asked about the negotiations earlier, but now was clearly not the time. Ram expected her to get work done, not chitchat.

This wasn't a safe place for her — for any of the Seuturan captives. And the longing for home was almost a physical ache inside her. She wanted solid ground under her feet and mountain air in her lungs.

Chapter 9

A week later, she still hadn't heard anything about the negotiations. Every time she asked, Ram told her he had no news about it. At the moment she was working beside Ram in what he told her was the maintenance bay, which was much smaller than the bay they'd arrived in, readying herself to pester him again about it. She had adjusted to the routine in the last week — Ram would have training most mornings, and then they would work on an assigned project or task each afternoon. He had one day off each week, and during this week's he had taken her to see the onboard garden.

He continued to treat her kindly, though he could be infuriating at times. Her mind kept going back to the negotiations, while Ram seemed so nonchalant about them. He had to know how important they were to her, but he never brought them up, leaving her to have to ask him about them again and again. And while the routine of knowing what would happen each day was soothing in some ways to her, there was such a deep, longing ache inside her for home.

Today they'd been assigned to help with the repairs on the transport that had been damaged during the attack. Lettering in large, red letters along the side of the vessel read *VTX-Rhincodon*. There was a small crew of maintenance personnel working on the damaged transport, but other than that it was empty and peaceful. She and Ram were cleaning the area where the damage was worst, at one of the lower-back engines. Blackened scoring on the hull and a jagged, gaping hole revealed the scorched inside of the engine.

She felt a surge of satisfaction when she saw the weapon damage to the transport — at least Seutura had put up a bit of a fight — but that was soon tempered with the knowledge that her own people had been on board when the damage occurred. She remembered initially thinking it would have been better to be shot down than in Varusian hands, but the worst of her fears of captivity hadn't come true. She found herself grateful for Varus' well-built ships.

Her second night onboard she had put the chair back in front of the door of her room. That time, though, she'd figured out how to set an alarm using the bedside table, so she'd been able to move it back before Ram opened the door in the morning. Ram had still given her a skeptical look when he fetched her for breakfast — as if he knew exactly what she had done — but didn't comment on it. After that night, she decided it wasn't worth the effort. He'd had plenty of opportunity to do something to her if he had wanted to.

She did notice that though Ram didn't always lock the door to her quarters, he kept the outer door locked with a code at all times.

Carina had seen a number of other Seuturan prisoners at meals and during work throughout the week. At meals the women were all in similar style dresses and the men wore similarly colored jumpsuits that had solid golden colored embellishments around the collar and wrists, and during work, they had the same red jumpsuits she wore. But Ram had steered her well clear of them. She both longed and feared to talk to them. Would one of them have more news than Ram told her? Would it be good news or bad? Would they be so concerned about their own problems that they wouldn't care for her questions?

She felt so out of sorts. She thrived on her steady, unchanging routine at home. Being thrust into a new situation, under difficult circumstances, had thrown her off. And it wasn't like she wanted to settle into a routine here. She didn't want to get used to this — hopefully she would be headed home in a few days.

She was actually incredibly thankful for the physical labor. It was easy compared to what she was used to, but having something for her hands to do, physical activity for her body, kept her centered.

She found herself eyeing the *Rhincodon* longingly. If only she could just hop on the ship and fly back down to Seutura and home. But this ship was definitely unflyable in its current state. The broken engine was already mostly dismantled, and most of the parts mangled or destroyed. Even to her untrained eye, she could tell it might be weeks or months before it was repaired.

It was strange to think it had already been a week since her capture. The days felt both infinitely long and yet so short. There hadn't been so much as a whisper as far as negotiations were going. But surely they had to have started by now.

Carina paused her work — she'd been scouring a blackened section of the transport's underside — and looked over at Ram. How he still managed to look good in the cleaning gear was beyond her. Though she was more than a little irritated to find herself noticing his looks.

"Have you heard anything?" she called out to him.

He raised his goggles up to the top of his head, pushing his brown hair back in a messy array.

"'Bout what, Buttercup?"

She gritted her teeth, but held her frustration in check. Why he insisted on calling her that ridiculous nickname was a mystery, other than the fact that he appeared to delight in her annoyance. She'd resolved to react less so as not to give him the satisfaction.

"The negotiations. Do I get to go home soon?" she asked, proud that she managed to keep her irritation from her voice.

"Haven't heard a thing. I'm sure it won't be long though." He slid the goggles back down over his eyes. "You know how these upper-ups love to chat. It's only been a week. Just be patient." He turned back to continue air blasting a section of the engine casing.

She let out a long sigh, and went back to her own work. Patient. She just had to be patient. She could go back home soon.

Carina turned the nozzle setting on the spout up a couple notches and blasted at the under-casing, grateful she could at least take out her frustration on something. She swiped the blast of air back and forth over the metal in front of her.

The blast of air must have caught one of the twisted pipes in just the wrong way, because a piece of metal shot off with a *twang*. A stream of black oil spurted out from the engine casing...

And straight onto Ram, splattering him all over.

She released the handle of her air nozzle, abruptly stopping the air flow, and her eyes went wide.

Ram cut his hose's air flow off, and he turned very slowly toward her. He reached down with a hand and swiped some of the oil off his jumpsuit.

"I am so sorry," Carina said, clutching her hose as she felt both the irrational urge to giggle and a small jolt of alarm. Did he think she'd done it on purpose? Before she could stammer out an explanation, he flung his hose down and dashed for her.

She let out a pathetic scream, though it wasn't true fear — she didn't think Ram would *really* hurt her. She dropped her own cleaning tools and turned to dart away. Where she thought she might go, she had no idea. Before she could take three steps Ram was already on her, clutching her around the middle.

His arms firmly grasped her. She shrieked, and tried to wheeze out another apology — then she realized he was chuckling, and there really was no anger in his actions. She tried to calm herself.

"Put me down," she managed to get out.

"You want me to put you down?" he asked, his voice rumbling in a playful tone in her ear. He began walking over to where he had been standing.

"Wait!" she protested, struggling against him.

"Oh, no, Buttercup," Ram said. "I think it's only fair we match."

"Wait, it was an accident!" she said, then gave another shriek as he deposited her onto the puddle of oil. The stream coming from the ship had slowed down, but there was still plenty pouring over her. It smelled horrible. "Ugh!" She looked up to where Ram was grinning above her, and even through the goggles she could see his eyes crinkled in true amusement. She glared up at him.

He chuckled again.

She scooped some of the oil as best she could in her hand and hurled it at his still grinning face. It splattered all over nose and mouth and she was rewarded by the shocked expression on his face. She let out a loud laugh.

That brought attention from others working on the ship. She felt suddenly self conscious. Dozens of workers were staring at the two of them. Ram glanced around, before offering her a hand up. His hand was firm and warm, but because of the oil, his grip slipped before she could get her feet firmly under her.

Eventually he carefully reached down and picked her up — not too unlike how he carried her to the processing center — and gently set her down on her feet. The oil had soaked into both her jumpsuit and Ram's uniform.

"Damn the Founders," he muttered, looking down at his uniform. "This is never going to come out."

She felt the urge to giggle again. But with everyone staring at them, she stifled it quickly and tried to get back to work. Ram joined her, still muttering under his breath.

The oil made the rest of their work harder, and they had to hurry to complete it all in the allotted time. She had hoped to get to see more of her people at dinner time, but it took a good thirty minutes of showering to get all the foul oil out. By the time they had arrived, the mess hall was mostly empty, and while she saw a couple Seuturans, Ram sat at a table away from anyone else.

She felt herself regarding him differently that evening. He had washed up too, and something about him looked extra sharp. His hair was still as messy as usual, a mighty feat for how short it was. As they ate, he gave her a knowing grin. It was different from his normal grin, warmer and more friendly.

She was tempted to say something with him, to strike up a conversation, but then she was reminded of her still unanswered questions, and her mood soured. As amusing as the diversion with Ram had been, he was still her captor. She couldn't let herself get distracted. She was desperate for any word about the negotiations and hoped she would hear something soon. She resolved to be patient, and not to ask Ram about it. After all, he was Varusian. Who knew if he would tell her the truth?

Chapter 10

Carina's resolve to be patient was tested several days later when she overheard two of Ram's squadmates talking.

They were all eating lunch together at one of the long tables in the mess hall. Carina was enjoying her meal immensely — chicken and mushroom soup in a delicious bread bowl. She still couldn't get over how good their food on board was. Part of her wanted to ask Ram about it, but she disliked the idea of showing too much interest in his people or culture.

While she was contemplating how she might pull a recipe like this one off, she heard Feingo mention something about the diplomacy talks.

"Have you heard something?" she asked, then blushed slightly as both Feingo and the squadmate he was talking with turned their attention to her. She hadn't interacted much with the others in the squad, besides polite greetings and a few pleasantries. She only knew Feingo's name because he was who Ram sparred with the most, and had recognized his voice as one of the soldiers from the ship that transported her up to the *Architeuthis*. The rest of the squad seemed nice enough. They were courteous to her, and none of them had made her uncomfortable. Well, besides Thekla, who downright terrified her. But she was able to mostly steer clear of him. Feingo had even made her smile a time or two with his jokes.

Feingo hesitated, glancing at Ram, who gave him a look she couldn't decipher.

"Just that they're talking," Feingo said. "Nothing official." He gave her an apologetic look.

She nodded, trying not to feel discouraged.

"What are the Varusians trying to negotiate for anyways?" she asked.

"Reparations," Ram said quickly. There was an edge to his voice.

"Reparations for what?" she asked.

"Don't worry, Buttercup," Ram said, his voice softening a bit. "Just enjoy your time here with us. Well, most of us. Don't know if you noticed, but Alex here is a cranky old man most of the time."

Alex, who was the stern soldier Carina had encountered first on their shuttle ride up, gave Ram a harsh look that would have sent lesser men running.

"Some of us have to maintain discipline when Thekla isn't around," he quipped back.

"Thekla doesn't need any help with that," Ram replied. "He probably is twitching behind the ears, sensing that we're having a modicum of fun. If anything, that's what he, and you, need."

With that, the table devolved into a warzone of insults. At first she stared wide-eyed at the soldiers, until she realized how playful the banter was. The teasing was surprisingly friendly under the surface. Once she knew it wasn't going to escalate into a brawl, she paid it no mind.

Of course she had to expect the peace talks would take time. When did politicians and leaders ever move quickly with things, especially when they weren't personally affected? The Varusians should have grabbed some of the leader's families — *that* would have expedited the negotiations. She immediately regretted that thought, ashamed it had even popped into her head.

Though, if she was honest with herself, she was beginning to have doubts that the war was even real. She couldn't imagine anything big enough to instigate a war happening that they would have heard nothing about at the Intrepid colony. Even as far out as they were, rumors traveled faster than official news. And what was there to fight over anyway? From the technology she saw on board, and the food they ate, it seemed like they were far better off on Varus than Seutura. What could they possibly hope to gain by going to war with Seutura?

Perhaps the Varusians had just invented a reason to start things. *Reparations*, Ram had said. For what? *Existing*? Her time among the Varusians hadn't been horrible, which had cast doubt on the rumors she'd heard growing up that they were war-mongering barbarians. They seemed civilized enough to her, but they *had* captured Seuturan hostages, so that wasn't saying much. Maybe they were set on conquering them.

And she certainly wasn't going to enjoy her time here, like Ram suggested. Keep her head down and survive it, yes. But there was nothing to enjoy about being a war prisoner. Well, she inwardly amended as she took another bite of bread dipped in soup, except perhaps the food.

But the yearning for home was an aching pit inside of her. Her colony, the mountains, the mines even. Her chats and times of laughter with Bryn. The comforting routine and flow of each day, each week. All that was familiar to her. She missed all of it.

She might even see if Tennel would agree to get married immediately when she got back. And if not immediately, then as soon as possible. She had started to wonder if he would still want her when she returned. There was the chance he might count her too contaminated by the experience. She wasn't sure what to think. Nothing like this had ever happened before, but there was an attitude of disgust towards anything Verusian back on Seutura, and any change was viewed with suspicion at her colony.

Well, she thought, thinking back to Bryn's teasing comments, perhaps it would be nothing a few loaves of nicely baked bread wouldn't fix.

She longed to return to her life, to continue on her planned course, even if there were a few small bumps getting it back on track.

But, strangely the thought that saddened her the most, was that her few herb plants would most likely all be dead by the time she returned home.

Chapter 11

His Buttercup was fading. That was the thought that came to Ram as he watched her, sitting on the couch in his quarters after dinner, staring blankly at the display scene, which currently cycled through some holophotos from Varus. It had been just under three weeks since they'd successfully pulled off the attack on Seutura. He found himself surprised at how well he'd settled into having Carina with him.

He was working on some reports on his tablet at the table in the corner. He was behind on a few things, and trying to get caught up for the week. And it didn't help any that he kept glancing up to peek at Carina.

He had noticed the problem shortly after their day working on the *Rhincodon*. At first, he'd thought the day was a turning point to her accepting her time here. What he would do to hear her laugh like that again. Getting covered with oil was a fair price to pay.

But instead, it seemed to be a different turning point. Just days after, she had withdrawn again. Even the small progress they made that first week evaporated quickly. He wasn't sure how to fix her. He had tried to show her around various areas on board the ship, when he wasn't training or they weren't doing their assigned tasks.

He'd even tried taking her to the small, on-board garden to cheer her up. She'd asked about their food — seemed amazed by it. In fact, it was almost the only thing she'd shown an interest in, besides her incessant questions about the diplomacy talks. When he'd explained how they stored food, and that they also had a small garden on board with a selection of plants from Varus, she'd perked up immediately.

It wasn't large, but they had quite a few types of plants and artificial sunlight shining down. Carina's face when he'd first brought her in was one of the most beautiful things he'd ever seen. He'd told her about the plants he knew about, mostly thanks to his mother's gardening growing up, and also about the large public gardens and enormous, wild forests on Varus.

But as much as she'd enjoyed it, she almost seemed more sad after. *Baffling, Seuturan woman.*

She did seem to enjoy the duties she had to perform, which surprised him at first, but then again she was used to long, hard days of labor in the mines. This must seem like a vacation compared to them. He'd tried to introduce her to other members of his squad, as well as other crew members he knew, during meals. She was never rude to them, but she remained reserved.

And she repeatedly asked about the negotiations. It made sense, of course, why she was so eager to know. But he'd heard nothing official yet, only rumors and hearsay which unfortunately didn't sound promising. He didn't want to tell her about those, however, and dash her hopes. All he could tell her was that he had no idea what the time frame would be, which seemed to leave Carina even more frustrated and withdrawn.

Ram knew he shouldn't care. She was a prisoner of war. A captive in his care. He was to make sure she was taken care of and that no harm came to her, but that didn't extend to making sure she was happy. In fact, he ought to be glad she was miserable. There were plenty of miserable Varusians who had lost loved ones. It was how this whole mess had started in the first place. He, of all people, should *especially* not care.

He should enjoy having a captive, be glad he had a chance to help further the war efforts and atone for his own failings.

And yet…he wrestled with this irrational urge to make her happy. To bring a smile to her face. The voice of his sister echoed in his head. In his mind, he could hear just what she would have said: *Make her happy.* He shook his head. It was a betrayal of those who had died.

Ram remained conflicted, vacillating between worry and determination to stay distant. He would have stayed there except for an incident one afternoon after a simulated battle training session with his squad.

Carina was helping him clean each armor piece and put it back away. She always worked so quietly and methodically. Ram sometimes found himself staring more at her, loose blonde locks of hair that had escaped her braid falling down over her face that was concentrated on the task in front of her. Feingo had joked that she was getting faster at taking care of his armor than he was. He'd gotten a good pummeling during training for that one.

But today was different. Carina was working on a particularly tough spot — he'd gotten a bit of blood on his right shoulder pad when one of his rolls had been slightly off, and he'd caught a training spear to the face. His chin was still aching from that one.

Carina abruptly stopped her work and stood up.

"Where you headed, Buttercup?" Ram asked, glancing up from the leg piece he'd been trying to work on while he watched her.

"I'm done."

Ram looked pointedly at the still bloody armor piece she'd dropped on the bench. "Doesn't look like it."

She huffed. But she didn't look very angry, which is what he had expected. In fact, her face held more of the fear that had possessed her during her initial day here. It gave him pause.

"No, I'm done." It was a statement of fact. Her hands, now clenched into fists, were shaking. He carefully set the armor piece in his hands down on the bench, but remained seated. She looked like she was close to full-blown panic, and he didn't want to spook her. Something had gotten into her, and he wasn't sure what.

"Okay, Buttercup," he said quietly. "We can be done."

"Stop calling me that!" She looked anguished as her voice rose for the first time in the conversation. "I'm not your blasted Buttercup. I don't want to be your captive, or hostage, or whatever you want to call it. I want to go home!"

At this outburst, she turned toward the door. Ram felt a jolt of fear and panic shoot through him. He had to regain control of the situation, but he didn't know how. If he was shown to not be able to control the captive he was in charge of, she'd get assigned to someone else. Grabbing her would just reinforce what she was thinking, but letting her run free on the ship...Mikael wasn't the only monster roaming around.

He found himself moving before he'd fully thought through what he planned. He vaulted over the bench, reached for her and then drew her firmly against his chest, trying to calm the fear inside himself. The adrenaline jolt of what might happen if she ran out had felt almost like he was going into battle.

Carina shook in his arms — sobbing, he realized. Instinctively, without even knowing why, he tucked her head against his chest just below his chin, and began to gently rub her back.

Her hair smelled nice, like blooming tsyr flowers in warm sunshine. It was a thought that came unbidden in the moment, and he felt annoyed at himself for noticing it, especially when she was clearly grieving. He knew grief — the heart wrenching sobs and pain that cut so deep, it felt as if he'd taken a blow from a stun staff.

Was that why he held her — comforted her? Because he wanted desperately to take away her pain, just as he'd longed for someone to take away his own. Both sides of that thought were unbefitting a soldier, but it stuck in his head. He didn't know why he just didn't let her be. Sobbing or not, it was her own people that had caused his pain, his grief, along with that of so many Varusians. She was a captive. And they had taken captives for a reason.

And yet...he still didn't let her go, comfortingly running his hands through her hair and down her back, while she clung to him — the very one who'd taken her captive in the first place.

And wondered what in the galaxy he was going to do now.

Chapter 12

Ram was taking her somewhere new, Carina realized. But exhaustion had seeped into every part of her being, and she couldn't muster any enthusiasm. He'd already shown her several areas of the ship, and they'd visited the star observatory several more times. They'd fallen into a comfortable routine in the roughly three weeks since she'd been taken — something that she hated, since she didn't want to be here in the first place. But there was this yawning pit inside her that just kept growing.

She still couldn't believe she'd snapped at him yesterday and tried to run. *Run.* Not that it had really been a run — he'd caught her before she had even fully realized she'd intended to flee. And she'd clung to him while she cried. She knew the thought should disgust her. It was all his fault she was even here to begin with. But it had felt good to be held, to be comforted against his warm, solid chest. Not that it had lasted long. Almost as soon as he had let her go and her tears dried, the pit took even those emotions. She couldn't even muster anger towards herself at enjoying Ram's touch. All she felt was numbness.

And where had she thought she could run to, anyway? As much as he'd shown her the ship, it was massive, and most of it was still a complete mystery to her. She was only just starting to memorize the route from the quarters to the mess hall.

If she made it to one of the hangars, what did she plan on doing? Walk up to the soldiers guarding it and ask very nicely if she could borrow one of their transport ships that she had no hopes of flying in any case?

As she followed Ram along the unfamiliar walkway she wondered if he had finally realized he'd gotten a defective captive. Maybe he was returning her. Maybe he'd pick someone new — someone adventurous and bubbly. The thought brought an uncomfortable pang of anger and jealousy. Which was ridiculous, of course. She should be thrilled he was returning her. She'd get away from him and his infuriating grins and nicknames. She'd get to be back with her own people, even if she would still be stuck on this ship.

When they reached a junction in the corridors he took her through a set of heavy doors. Ahead it looked as if the ship had been turned sideways. A long, tube-shaped tunnel lay ahead, but it was round with no apparent place to walk through.

"Here, you'll need this," Ram said, handing her what looked like a harness. His voice was level. Solemn even. It made her uneasy. He wore his full armor today, and even had his various weapons in their respective holsters. She wasn't suicidal enough to try to grab one. They looked very secure, it would take longer than a moment to pull one out. She realized the Varusian soldier in the hangar hadn't secured his blaster as well as Ram had. Had he wanted the captive to grab for it or had he just forgotten to secure it during the heat of the abduction mission? Which was the other reason she didn't try to grab Ram's weapons. She doubted he would try to kill her like the soldier had with the captive, but she wouldn't know how to activate or fire a blaster even if she took it. It was pointless.

He explained succinctly how to put the harness on. He didn't try to help or touch her. He'd been different today — without his usual grins. His appetite at breakfast had been far less than usual. And his regular morning training had been cut short.

Once the harness was on, he hooked her to a line that she saw ran along the side of the tube. Another thought struck her. It terrified her.

"Where are we going?" Carina managed to force the question out.

"You'll see." Vague. Solemn.

She blinked back tears, angry at herself for not being stronger. "Are you—" her voice broke, and she tried again. "Am I going to be executed?"

"What?" Ram stopped abruptly, and looked at her with utter bafflement.

She felt a tear fall, and swiped angrily at it. "What kind of place are you taking me? Are they going to execute hostages, or am I going to be beaten?"

Ram looked at her with horror. "How in the black void of the galaxy did you come to that conclusion?"

She looked around them uncertainly. "I've never seen anything like this in the ship before. And you seem...off." Carina looked up at him accusingly. "You didn't have your usual breakfast."

Ram shook his head, letting out a half laugh. "So you thought I was going to bring you to your death?" He cursed, and muttered something about listening to Feingo. "Come on." He strapped himself in on the line in front of her. He didn't need a harness because his armor had a place for a line from the wall to clip in. He grabbed her arm, a gentle, firm grip, and tugged her along. "Try not to let your imagination run any more rampant in the next two minutes."

Once they were through the door, it felt like everything turned sideways. Or upside down. She tried to orient herself or wrap her mind around the feeling but she couldn't.

"Just a little zero-g," Ram said, showing a small smile for the first time that morning. She looked down. She was floating. She had touched the edge of the tube as she had stepped out, but her motion had pushed her up off the ground and there was no gravity to cause her to return.

"What's going on?" she asked, looking around. She chided herself for that. Did she think someone was going to appear from nowhere and say 'gotcha!'?

"We have to pass through the zero-g section of the ship," Ram answered. He pulled her close, keeping their tethered lines near each other. She stiffened, but he seemed to ignore it. He reached out with one hand and pushed a button on the wall. She flinched and reflexively grabbed a hold of Ram as the line they were both attached to started dragging them along the tube. She clung to him, and caught a whiff of cloves with a hint of citrus.

As they accelerated, she felt an unfamiliar feeling, but once they were going, it felt rather pleasant. The tube was clear and she could see into the space around her, but all she could make out was what looked like storage areas in all directions. Crates upon crates were everywhere in an area even larger than the hangar. There was no orientation though. The crates looked as if they were either floating or strapped to any surface, floor, wall or ceiling without discrimination.

"Why does the ship have a zero-g section? *How* does it have a zero-g section?" she asked as they floated along.

"Classified and classified," Ram answered. "But why do you think we feel gravity on most of the ship?"

She tried to remember what she knew about some of the Seutran ships. "Rotation, right?"

Ram shook his head. "Does the ship look cylindrical to you?"

She was about to reply that she didn't exactly get a good look on their shuttle trip, but then she thought about what she did know about the layout. There definitely weren't sloping floors like it would need for rotation to give gravity.

"But wait...how does that work?" she said.

"Classified," he answered again with a grin. She just sighed, the curiosity fading away. Was it even a mystery worth trying to solve at this point?

The tube ride ended quickly, and after a short deceleration and Ram helping her to the end, they were back in normal gravity. From there it was just a short walk to their destination. Heavily armed guards stood at attention beside a large hatch, two large, thick glass windows at either side. They nodded at Ram, as if they were expecting him, and one reached over to type something into the keypad beside him. She hadn't seen security anywhere near like this anywhere else on the ship.

The hatch slid open, revealing another set of guards and yet another hatch. Through a window beside the door, she glimpsed a small room of women, all dressed in what she'd come to recognize as Varusian clothing for the captives.

She shot a confused look at Ram, but he was talking quietly to the guards. Then one keyed something into the keypad, and the thick door slid open. Many of the women turned to look at them as the hatch opened up. Some looked warily, others indifferent. Most turned quickly back to whatever they were doing. There were about a dozen tables spread throughout the room and about the same number of couches along the walls. It was larger than it had appeared through the window, so it wasn't cramped, though it wasn't spacious either. Most of the tables were filled, but a few stood empty. Each group of women seemed to be doing their own thing. Some talking, some just sitting together. She noticed one woman with an array of curly red hair perk up when she spotted Carina.

Ram put a hand on her lower back and pushed her gently forward. She glanced back at him.

"Fifteen minutes," he said.

"But, wait— are—"

"Fifteen minutes, Buttercup," he interrupted, giving her a warning look. "Don't waste them."

She turned and took hesitant steps toward the women, feeling suddenly self-conscious. The door slid closed behind her. Through the window, she saw Ram cross his arms and lean against the bulkhead. He gave a quick glance in, but seemed to be conversing with the guards outside.

She stood there a moment, unsure of what to do. She scanned the faces of the captives, but didn't recognize anyone. It was a large room and many of the women had their backs turned to her. She chided herself for wishing she had spotted Bryn. Her *not* being here was a good sign, she reminded herself. It meant she most likely had escaped. She remained unsure of what to do or who to even try to approach, until a younger woman with long brown hair came up to her.

"Hey there," she said with a kind smile. "I'm Kimura."

"Carina," she answered, feeling uncertain. Besides Ram's squad — which to her didn't count — it had been years since she had to introduce herself in a room where she knew almost no one. The colony of Intrepid was small enough that everyone knew everyone.

Kimura saved her from the awkward silence. "Want to come join us?" she asked, gesturing to a table with several women sitting around it. "Where are you from?"

"Intrepid," Carina answered as she followed Kimura. "It's a small colony in Encadus. We run the big titanium mine in the area."

Kimura smiled. "Well, I hadn't heard of it before I was brought up here, but at this point I know pretty much every place they took hostages from. It must have been significant if the Varusians attacked it."

That made sense. Of course they would have taken captives from key targets. Carina wasn't sure of the total number of people that had been taken captive, but she remembered the vast number of shuttles landing in the hangar on that first day.

Kimura led her over to the table where a small group of women sat. "That's Shaian," Kimura said, gesturing to a woman who looked to be in her thirties, with dark blonde hair that ended at her shoulders. "And that's Triska and Niki." She pointed as she said each name. "And this, ladies, is Carina."

They all greeted her as she approached, but she saw a wariness in some of their expressions.

"Are any of you assigned, or—" Carina began to ask, but figured she knew the answer. She had never seen this many Seuturans together in one place on the *Architeuthis*, not even when the mess hall was at its fullest. She remembered what Ram had said about them only assigning some of the captives to the crew.

"Oh, no," Triska said, shaking her head. She was the same curly red head that had perked up when Carina had first entered the room. The act of shaking her head set her curls into motion that took a moment to slow to a stop. She seemed the most lively of the group. "We've just been kept here with a group of the other women. They have us divided into sections."

"How many sections?" Carina asked. There were well more than fifty women here, and this apparently was just one section of many.

"I believe there are eight to ten sections for just the women like this," Shaian answered. She spoke in the tones of someone who brooked no nonsense. "If the men are in a similar setup as us, plus the ones like you—" she gestured at Carina, indicating those who were assigned to a Varusian "—my best estimate is that there are about a thousand hostages total on board."

The way Shaian gestured at her made Carina draw back half a step, folding her arms around her. She felt like an outsider at that moment. As if her time with Ram had tainted her. It was subtle in Shaian's attitude, not something overt, but there nonetheless.

"Carina Mosaido?" Carina turned as she heard the voice calling her name from behind her.

She recognized her instantly — it was one of the older women from her colony, gray hair clipped short and the lines on her telling not only her age but the toll the mines had taken on her. "Yeunay?"

The older woman immediately enveloped her in a hug. They weren't very close, but Yeunay had known Carina's mother, and had checked in on her from time to time. And it felt comforting to see someone familiar in this strange place.

"Sorry to see you got snagged too," Yeunay said, pulling back and giving her a look over.

"Have you seen Bryn?"

Yeunay shook her head. "Nah, but that doesn't mean much. They jumbled us all up pretty good."

"Come, sit," Shaian said to both of them, her voice a shade warmer than a moment ago. "You know Yeunay? Glad you found someone you know from home."

"I've known Carian since I could bounce her on my knee, Shaian. She's reliable and a hard worker."

"And you're looking for someone else?" Shaian asked.

"Another woman from our colony — Bryn Gaudin," Carina said, taking a seat. Yeunay sat next to her. "I'm not even sure she's here. She was on the same transport as we were, but I didn't see what happened in the chaos."

"I haven't seen her, but I haven't seen anyone outside of this room," Yeunay said. "Maybe she got away."

"I'll ask around just to check," Shaian said, "and see what I can find out. It's the least I can do for a friend of Yeunay."

"Thank you." Carina looked around at the group. "How are they treating all of you?"

"No complaints on the accommodations," Triska said. It seemed every movement and gesture highlighted her hair. Each curl seemed to move about on its own volition. Carina was jealous — which was foolish in the situation they were in — of how full her curls were. She knew they could be a pain to work with, but they looked spectacular on the woman.

"And the guards have kept their hands to themselves," Niki added quietly. She seemed more reserved than the others, and also younger. Even the way she sat, almost hiding behind Shaian, made her seem to fade into the background.

"Except for that incident the first night," Kimura said. "But it seems the instigators were dealt with."

"Except that." Niki nodded. "But we've been well taken care of. I have to say in some ways it's better than back home."

After meeting Mikael, Carina was not surprised there had been an incident. She hoped there wouldn't be any more. She had to admit that Mikael seemed to be in the minority of the Varusians, even though she would never say that outloud to Ram.

Niki's sentiment, however, surprised Carina. Even if it was true that some of the conditions were better, there was no way Carina would admit it. Apparently she wasn't the only one who thought that way.

"Don't say that, my dear!" Shaian said with just a bit of sharpness. Niki flinched back, and Carina thought for a moment her feelings had been hurt. But then she nodded, as if agreeing with the admonishment. "Seutura might lack some of these amenities, but the one thing it definitely lacks is the cages we are in."

Yeunay grunted in agreement. "Barbarians." She looked at Carina. "They treating you okay?"

"She means those out there," Shaian explained, gesturing beyond the doors, although Carina was sure Yeunay was just asking about her. Yeunay gave a small shrug as Shaian continued. "We haven't seen many of the captives who have been assigned to the *crew*."

The way she intoned the word *crew* left an unspoken statement in the air. If a shy girl such as Niki could state the praises of being here, what would Carina say, who has been mingling with the Varusians.

"My soldier has been...nice," Carina said carefully. *Nice* wasn't really the way to describe Ram, but she couldn't think of what else to say. That earned her a look from Shaian and a grunt from Yeunay. "He has," she continued with a shrug. "I've mostly been helping him with ship tasks. Not saying I like it here or anything, but as gruff as he can be, I have to admit he's been courteous."

"Hmm, I wouldn't mind if some of these guys were less courteous," Triska said with a smirk.

Carina blushed. Kimura gave Triska a look and a small shove on the shoulder. "Triska!"

"What?" Triska asked, shrugging. "Have you *seen* the muscles on these guys? And they seem nice enough. Just saying..."

"We're *prisoners* of war," Shaian said, leveling a look at Triska that was equal parts admonishment and disgust. Yeunay muttered something under her breath about "the idiocy of youth."

Triska humphed. "Doesn't mean we need to be miserable."

There was a loud tap on the window. Carina glanced over, and saw Ram hold up five fingers.

"Do you have access to anything critical?" Shaian asked her quickly, in an even lower voice.

Carina's brow furrowed. "Like what?"

"Anything," Shaian said, glancing briefly at the glass windows. "Information. Equipment. Weapons."

"Not really," Carina said. "I go with him to their squad locker room, but their weapons are always locked up or on them. They'd know in an instant if I took something. And he's always with me around the armor." She frowned. "Why?"

Shaian glanced around at the other women, her gaze stopping on Yeunay who gave her a nod. "A few of us are planning an escape."

"But...I mean, the negotiations," Carina started to say. Not that escape hadn't occurred to her, of course. But it seemed risky, especially considering there were negotiations ongoing. She wouldn't want to do something that might disrupt them and put others in danger.

Shaian shook her head. "We can't wait for the bureaucrats to sort things out. Trust me." She leaned closer. "I have contact with the men, because one of them is allowed to come visit his wife who was also taken. There are solid groups on both sides who want in." Shaian seemed used to being in charge. If her comment on the bureaucrats was from experience, Carian could believe she not only knew how to lead, but also seemed like she had a steady head on her shoulders. Carina felt a sudden pang of sadness, wishing desperately she could stay here with these women and Yeunay, who she actually knew, instead of isolated from her people.

"Not everyone?" Carina asked, hugging herself tightly as nervous energy buzzed through her. Escape. Hope surged in her. Someone was planning an escape. And if they pooled their minds and resources together, maybe they could pull it off. Shaian certainly seemed confident enough.

"Some of us are content to stay," Triska said, leaning back in the seat.

Carina looked at her, *aghast*. "You want to stay?"

Triska shrugged. "It's not like my life back on Seutura was great anyway. I worked as an underappreciated and underpaid farmer, shoveling manure into soil that doesn't want to be planted in any way. My parents are dead — I've got basically no one. I'm ready for a nicer life, and to not smell like crap all day. And there are a few who are content. Not that any of us will interfere," she hastened to add, glancing at Shaian, who looked grim.

Carina knew their circumstances on Seutura weren't amazing. But she couldn't imagine anyone wanting to leave their home and people, even for better conditions. Especially not to live among an unknown people and culture. She just couldn't wrap her head around it.

"So, are you in or not?" Shaian asked Carina. "We can't take everyone, but I have to admit, you who are out there—" she gestured at the door "—have a better chance than most of us in here to get out. You're already past the hard part."

"Yes, of course," Carina said. "I want to go home."

Shaian nodded. "Just keep your ears and eyes open." She glanced back at Ram. "Think he'll bring you here again?"

"Um, maybe?" Carina shrugged, glancing at Yeunay. "But I'll try."

"We'll keep you in the loop as much as we can," Yeunay said quietly. She glanced over Carina's shoulder, scowled and crossed her arms. Triska looked in the same direction and broke into a broad smile.

"Time to go," Ram said firmly from behind her. She had missed the sound of the door opening and his approach. Carina quietly said farewell to the women. But for the first time since her capture, she felt true hope bloom inside her.

Chapter 13

"You're happier."

Ram's words startled her, and she nearly dropped the roll of sealant tape she was holding. They were currently cataloging and organizing one of the storage rooms on board. "What?"

He was watching her with curiosity, and something else she couldn't quite identify.

"Talking to your people. It helped."

"Um, yes. I guess so," she said hesitantly, her mind racing. Did he suspect they had talked about escape? They had tried to keep their conversation quiet, but maybe someone had overheard. She'd been paying attention more, though so far she hadn't found out anything that might be helpful. And she supposed she *had* been in much better spirits. She couldn't help it — the prospect of going home had given her fresh hope.

"Good." Ram looked pleased.

"Why?" she blurted out, and immediately regretted it.

Ram's brow furrowed. "Why what?"

"Why do you care?"

Ram bristled, slamming the storage cabinet closed. "Don't want my captive sulking around all day and refusing to work," he said, turning his attention to the remaining equipment.

Rolling her eyes, and unfooled by his deflection, she finished placing the sealant rolls in their container and slid it onto its shelf, then engaged the magnetic lock to keep it in place. She looked over as Ram picked up another spool of thermal conductive insulator and hefted it on its shelf. She found she enjoyed working with Ram when he wasn't outright annoying her — not that she would admit it outloud. He was a hard worker, and yet frequently managed to be entertaining. Despite her attempts not to smile — he really didn't need any more encouragement — she often couldn't resist.

The reminder of the women she'd met made her pause. "Could you...maybe see if a friend of mine is with the captives?"

"Who?"

"Her name is Bryn Gaudin. She was in the same transport I was in."

Ram looked at her impassively for a moment. "I'll see what I can do." He turned back to his work.

She hesitated a moment, wanting to ask another question, but also not wanting to push her luck. It was probably the best she could hope for, but she had to know if she'd be able to see the other women again, to have a chance at being in on the escape plans. "Also, um, could I visit the other women captives again sometime?" She hesitated a moment, then continued hastily, "One of the ladies there was from my colony. It was...nice to see someone I knew." She held her breath while she waited for his answer. If he didn't allow it, how would she know when the escape would be attempted?

He grunted, heaving a roll of conductive flexi-pipe up onto its rack. He kept his face turned away from her, and she got the impression it was on purpose. "Maybe," he said.

She let out her breath slowly and hid a grin. That was better than she had hoped.

*   *   *

Carina carried a warm cup of herbal tea that had a lid Ram had pilfered from somewhere as they made their way to the training center one morning. It had become part of the daily routine for her. The only time they didn't come here was Ram's one day off a week. She took a long sip of the tea, savoring the flavor.

Apparently, the last couple weeks she had been taking longer than he liked for her to finish her cup of tea each morning. There had been several mornings with Ram grumbling at her, and him constantly rushing her out of the mess before she had a chance to finish. And her suggestion that perhaps they get to breakfast fifteen minutes earlier had been met with outright incredulity. It seemed he had a set amount of time he thought breakfast should take.

So one morning she told him she wouldn't leave their table in the mess hall until she had finished her entire cup of tea. When he looked like he would combust on the spot she took the smallest sip possible, because at that point she was feeling irritated. He'd stood beside her, arms crossed and fuming for a minute before stalking off. He had threatened not to let her go visit the women again, but she was pretty sure he was bluffing, so she'd just ignored him and continued to sip at her tea.

When he returned, he grabbed her tea from in front of her. She thought he was going to pour it out, but instead he poured it into the cup she now used on a daily basis. He popped a lid on, handed it to her roughly, and huffed off without a word, his footsteps loud against the floor. That had received a few amused glances, and a teasing comment from Ram's friend Kovar that drew a curse from him.

It had made Ram late for training, which caused Thekla to give Ram twenty extra laps around the training room and locker bathroom cleaning duty for a week. He had been in a surly mood the rest of the day.

The next morning, Ram made sure she brought the tea cup with her to the mess hall and gave her the warning that if she ever made them late again, *she'd* be the one doing laps and he would definitely *not* let her visit the other prisoners again. She had solemnly agreed — after all, she had her tea.

"Why do you guys train all the time?" Carina asked as they neared the training room.

"Why wouldn't we train?" Ram seemed confused by her question.

"I mean," Carina said, gesturing at him, "you seem fine."

"Why, thank you for noticing." He winked at her with a small grin.

She sighed and rolled her eyes. "You all clearly already know how to fight. And it's not like you have anyone to fight right now."

"But we need to be ready."

"Why? It's not like Seutura has much of a fighting force anyways," she said, looking down at her cup. He made a disbelieving noise, which she ignored. "Besides, where did you learn all these fighting techniques anyway?"

Ram was quiet for a long moment as they rode in a lift down toward the training area. "Our planet has a rather tumultuous history," he said as they were almost at the entrance. "For a long time, we were split into various factions, and there was a lot of fighting among them. We can chat more later," he told her, sending her off to the alcove she normally sat in.

She rarely sat alone anymore — there were usually a couple Seuturans who joined her that had also been assigned to crew members who were training. She hadn't been brave enough to broach the topic of escape with them — if prisoners like Triska wanted to stay, she wasn't sure how these integrated prisoners would react. The irony was not lost on her. She chatted with them, and it was nice to commiserate, but she wasn't brave enough to open up to them completely.

Today she was half distracted, though, thinking about Ram's words. For as far back as she remembered learning about Seutura history, they'd been one, united government. There'd been plenty of disagreements, and often different goals for the planet, but overall everyone had stuck together. Sure, Seutura had its share of uprisings as well, but those had been put down to keep the collective peace. On such a harsh planet, it was a matter of survival.

There was so little she knew about Varus. Despite both planets existing in the same system, they might as well have been in different galaxies.

Half an hour into the training a broad shouldered man with blonde hair in a white officer's uniform entered the training room, and all of the soldiers shot to attention. Carina stiffened — remembering her only other encounter with an officer had been unpleasant.

"At ease," he called out, and made his way over to Ram's squad. The rest of the room quickly returned to their drills. She watched the man warily. The squad gave him a hearty greeting, however, and Ram even gave him a slap on the back with a broad smile. He seemed to have a good rapport with the men. She watched, curious, and tried to overhear what she could.

"You coming to join us, Halvar?" Thekla asked, breaking into a fierce grin. Carina nearly fell off her bench — she couldn't remember seeing Thekla smile before.

"He better," Ram said before the officer could speak up. "It's been so long since he last did that he'll be lucky to take down poor Kovar."

"Thanks for the support there, buddy," Kovar said, rolling his eyes.

"Of course I will," Halvar said with a grin. "Just let me warm up a little and I'll see if I can put our friend in his place."

He moved over to Carina and the other captives as he removed his outer officer's jacket and revealed some looser clothes. His gaze rested on Carina for a moment as he tossed his jacket on one of the benches, but she didn't get the feeling there was anything lewd about it. He just gave her an appraising look, then nodded, as if he'd solved a mystery. Her brow furrowed as he turned back to the training mat.

The next twenty minutes seemed mostly routine. Halvar joined the squad for some drills. His movements seemed rather crisp for an officer, although it wasn't like Carina had a lot of experience to draw from to be a good judge of that.

After that, however, things got interesting.

The training shifted into a dueling rotation. The squad broke up into groups and sparred, and then they rotated until each pair had faced each other. The rounds were quick, so as to not completely tire everyone out before they rotated through everyone, but Halvar seemed to get the upper hand easily against most of his opponents , and never lost as far as Carina could tell.

Members of the other squads started watching as Halvar faced opponent after opponent. At first it was just one or two soldiers, looking on while their squad leaders tried to bring their attention back to training. But soon more and more came to spectate, and eventually even the leaders joined them.

The squad leaders started gathering around Thekla, and Carina saw a wicked grin on his face. It was more frightening to her than when he had yelled at Ram her first day here. He whispered with the other squad leaders and eventually, after a lot of head nods and shakes, they seemed to come to an understanding.

What surprised Carina was that Thekla was looking at Ram as much as Halvar when he was grinning and talking.

Ram was also doing well. All the attention seemed focused on Halvar, but as far as Carina could tell, Ram hadn't lost a round either. When the last round finally matched

Ram against Halvar, she wondered if someone had set it up that way on purpose. The rest of Ram's squad stopped training as well and stood off to the side to watch. At first Carina was afraid she wouldn't be able to see it because of all the large soldiers standing in the way, but someone seemed to be mindful of those in the back, and had the first couple rows sit or kneel to watch.

The room was silent as the two faced off. The spars usually were so quick that there was little formality in them, but Ram and Halvar bowed and saluted before they fell into their stances. She had expected it to start slow, like they do in the holovid stories, but they were barely in their stances a moment before the action began. Halvar was the first to move, lashing out at Ram with a speed that made it nearly impossible to follow. Ram dodged, matching Halvar's speed and moving through the opening to get close and behind Halvar, but he seemed to anticipate the motion and lifted a foot to kick off Ram enough to get out of the way.

There was a cheer from the soldiers. The kick hadn't knocked Ram off balance, but Ram still hadn't been able to complete his take down. It seemed to Carina that for the soldiers this meant a point for Halvar. Both he and Ram paused enough after the exchange to give each other another salute before diving back into the thick of things.

There were three more bouts where neither seemed to get the advantage over the other. Each seemed to last longer than the last. Carina couldn't follow it all, but she could tell they weren't holding anything back. By the end of the third, both were dripping with sweat and Ram had stripped his shirt off at some point between rounds, revealing a well-muscled chest that she found annoyingly attractive. She tried not to let her eyes linger, focusing on the fight.

The next clash, she saw Halvar come in low, trying to sweep Ram's legs. Ram anticipated with a jump, and then pushed forward to grab Halvar's shirt, but Halvar instead used Ram's motion to move beside him. Carina thought Halvar was about to land a good blow, when Ram suddenly shifted to the side where Halvar was, in a motion that seemed to defy his bulk. Halvar swung an arm to counter, and landed a glancing blow on Ram's side but Ram's momentum was enough to knock Halvar solidly to the ground.

That seemed to end it, and the soldiers cheered even more loudly than they had before. Thekla's grin was even wider now, and she saw some of the other squad leaders grudgingly hand something over to him.

"You're lucky I don't have time to come down here and train more often, Ram," Halvar said, as Ram helped him up. "I used to be able to take you down any day of the week."

"It's alright, sir. I'm sure the papers they're having you push are downright scared after you return from getting your butt kicked." Halvar let out a curse, but was good natured. Both men went off, exchanging more remarks, and everyone else seemed to realize there were supposed to be more than two men training today. The squad leaders yelled at their respective squads. The ones that sounded the most irritated seemed to be the ones that had handed some sort of tokens to Thekla, but they all were trying to salvage the last few minutes of the session.

Carina was shocked at the comradery. She had seen it between Ram and his squad, but would never have expected it from an officer. They were all still Varusians, she reminded herself, but part of her had to accept that not all of those in white uniforms were entirely unredeemable.

Chapter 14

Ram didn't open up to her immediately about Varusian history after the training. They had to head down to the storage bay and help move some equipment needed for repairs on the damaged transport. It was only after they finished cleaning up that Ram took her to the ship garden and continued their conversation. She relaxed on one of the benches, looking around at the different plants and enjoying the artificial sunlight filtering through the glass dome above.

The garden amazed her. And what amazed her even more was what Ram had told her of Varus. Massive, wild forests, with such a variety of plants and animals. That many people kept beautiful, lush private gardens for themselves, not just for food but to grow beautiful flowers and a vast array of plants. She couldn't even begin to imagine what it might feel like to stand in a place like that, when even this onboard garden — which he called *small* — felt like a miracle to her.

Today she wore a dark blue chiffon dress that had a sleeveless bodice with a high collar. A sash-like belt made of the same material rested high on her waist. She played with the flowing pleats of the skirt while Ram, who sat sideways on the bench beside her, arms crossed, gazed out at the plants.

"Our planet's history is a rather complex one," he said. "I won't bore you with all the details, but the short version is this: decades ago the planet was split into five different major factions and far more minor ones, and that stretched back for several hundreds years or so. Things were even more chaotic before then." He shifted slightly on the bench. "There was lots of fighting amongst the factions. Occasionally there were periods of peace, but they were few and far between."

He paused, and gestured around them. "The blessing of that is our technology advanced rather rapidly, as factions sought to gain an advantage over one another. We made some technological advancements that only sped up that process. There was the occasional treaty between factions, though they tended not to last long. That changed," he said, looking at her, "roughly fifty years ago."

"What changed?" Carina thought back on the past fifty years of what she knew of Seuturan history. She couldn't think of anything remarkable happening, just the unceasing struggle to advance their agricultural techniques. She did remember as a young teen hearing about a mining strike at another mine across planet over working conditions, and some dissenting discussion in their own colony as to whether they would follow suit. When the other strike was quickly put to rest, discussion at Intrepid about striking had ceased, and never been brought up again.

Ram shrugged. "Grew tired of their differences, started setting their eyes on a bigger goal, finally pulled their heads out of their butts — who knows. The leaders of the five factions, plus a smattering of smaller ones, got together and formed a single government. And that's still in power to this day."

Carina frowned. "Just like that? Factions that had been warring for hundreds of years just suddenly decided to play nice?"

"Hey, if you want a historical analysis, talk to a historian," Ram said. "Just telling you what I know. In any case, the two most militaristic factions were the largest, Runak and Cortese. They joined to form the bulk of the army and fighting force. We have a large military, and we've been able to squash down any rebellions or people attempting to harm us."

"So, is there a president, or something like that?"

"We have a ruling family — Jethren Mallakis is currently the Imperator as he was the leader of Runak, though he doesn't hold exclusive power. There's a ruling counsel with him. Then there's the upper command of the military. They're the ones in the white uniforms you might see sometimes."

"Like that guy I met shortly after I came on board — Mikael, right?"

Ram's face tightened. "Yes, he's one of the upper command. But Admiral Untamo is in charge of the *Architeuthis* and this mission, and he's a good leader. We're not a perfect society," he admitted with a shrug. "We still have our share of problems."

She watched his face carefully, noting how the artificial sunlight reflected rather nicely of his green eyes.

"So we fight," Ram said. "To keep ourselves in top shape to prepare for the worst, for whatever we may face." He spoke with such conviction, an intensity to his face and words that she was slightly taken aback by.

"What made you attack Seutura?" she asked quietly, tilting her head so she could see him more clearly.

Instantly, the intense expression on his face morphed into anger. "We're not getting into that today."

"But—" she started to say, then broke off, recognizing the implacable expression on his face that meant the discussion was over. He had often made that exact face if she asked too often about the negotiations.

They were silent for a while, both staring off into the greenery around them. Most of the plants were unrecognizable to her. There was a section of edible plants Ram had pointed out to her, but she hadn't learned much about them yet.

"I could teach you."

Ram's words broke into the quiet and startled her. "What?"

"To fight. I could teach you."

Carina looked at him skeptically. "You could teach me how to fight?"

"Sure," he said, his gaze resting on her.

"What's the point? It's not like I'll ever need it." She tried to imagine herself moving like the soldiers she'd seen train, actually using those skills against another person. But it just didn't interest her.

"You don't know that."

Carina shook her head. "The diplomatic talks will end at some point, and I'll go back home and continue my life." Hopefully sooner, rather than later.

"In the mines," he said flatly. She couldn't read his expression.

"Yes. Well, for a while, but we were going to put in a request to transfer to a workplace in an agricultural district."

Ram's brow furrowed, and he cocked his head. "What do you mean 'we'?"

"Well," she said, flustered. She felt annoyed as the heat of a blush bloomed over her face. "Tennel. A guy. From the colony."

His eyes narrowed. "I didn't realize you were with someone. You haven't mentioned him before."

"We're not exactly...together." She felt frustrated with herself. She should never have brought him up. There was no reason Ram or anyone on this ship needed to know about Tennel. She didn't know why, but she felt awkward talking about him to Ram.

"What in the galaxy does that mean?"

Carina winced, surprised at his harsh tone. "We've agreed it would be beneficial to marry," she answered. "We would get allotted a better apartment, and a chance at better work."

Ram snorted. "That sounds like a business arrangement, not a marriage."

She rolled her eyes. "You sound like my friend Bryn. It's not like everyone can afford to be particular."

"Do you even like him?" Ram looked at her as though he thought she was crazy.

She scowled. "He's nice!"

"Nice? That's what you say when you don't know someone well enough to comment on them."

"He's nicer than barbarian soldiers who come and kidnap people."

Ram laughed out loud, dismissing her comment with a wave. "And that's the grand total you want from life — to work as a farmer, married to some guy you don't know—" Carina stiffened "—and never do anything exciting or worthwhile."

Arrogant ass. She sat up, fists clenched. "I don't *need* excitement. I don't *want* excitement. This little escapade on your Varusian ship is more excitement than I've ever wanted in my life. I can't wait to get back to my wonderful, *boring* life, and forget all about this."

She stood and stormed toward the exit of the garden. Dense, barbarian soldier. Flitting through life, one adventure to the next, no desire to take anything seriously. Except hitting people over the head and grabbing innocent people. Like that was a way to live. Of course she couldn't expect him to understand the practical considerations of her life — of the life of all Seuturans.

The negotiations better be done soon. Otherwise she might end up trying to find a rock on the ship and try hitting him when his helmet wasn't on.

Chapter 15

Ram was still debating whether he had lost his mind when he pounded on Carina's door at five-thirty in the morning. They had barely talked the rest of the day yesterday, but before going to bed he had decided on his course of action. He knocked again, and braced himself. He wondered why he felt more nervous doing this than going into battle.

The door slid open to reveal a very grouchy looking, and rather cute, Carina — though he'd go to his death before he'd reveal *that* thought — with hair disheveled, some strands of her golden blonde hair that had escaped from her braid cascading down the sides of her face. She was scowling, arms crossed, probably still ticked off from yesterday, even though he'd gotten her an extra helping of the chocolate cake she liked so much. He didn't regret what he'd said — he still thought the whole thing with this Tennel guy was idiotic. But the last thing he wanted was a sulky captive fouling up his mood. So he was going to fix things. That's the reason why he was doing this, he kept telling himself.

"Good morning, Buttercup."

Her scowl deepened even further. He hoped to the stars she never found out how adorable he thought it made her look. "Is there something wrong with my clock?" she asked, her voice still slightly gravelly from sleep.

"Put this on," he said, tossing her a slim, flexi tank top and pants he'd scrounged up in her size. She looked from him to the clothing, and back to him, and opened her mouth — likely to deliver a scathing remark. He interrupted her before she could speak — "Five minutes." Then he keyed the door shut in her face.

Four-and-a-half minutes later a fuming, but fully clothed, Carina exited her room. He led her, sputtering protests, out and to the dining hall where they ate a quick breakfast. Carina remained grumpy the whole time, though she grudgingly took the travel cup of tea with a muttered, "Thank you," when he handed it to her.

Ram was still in good spirits when he led her into the training room. It was mostly deserted — he only saw a guy from Delta squad practicing with a training dummy, and another crew member cleaning a section of flooring.

He had donned his usual sparring uniform. He took the travel mug from Carina — who uttered a protest — and set it by the benches in the observation alcove. Then he led her over to one of the smaller training circles.

"We need to stretch first," he told her, easing himself down onto the cushioned floor. "Not stretching before you practice is a good way to injure yourself."

Carina glared down at him. "Why are we here?"

"To teach you to fight," he said, moving into a gentle stretch. He motioned her to sit down too, but she didn't move.

"I don't need to know how to fight," she said, arms folded.

"Everyone should, at bare minimum, have some basic defense skills. To defend against idiots like Mikael."

She scoffed. "My world isn't nearly as dangerous as yours. And," she added, throwing him a challenging look, "I'll have Tennel to protect me."

Ram barely restrained a growl. Infuriating woman. It wasn't any of his concern if she wanted to get married as a business arrangement — hell, some marriages were made on far worse than that — but clearly she hardly knew the guy. She seemed to have this blasted optimistic view of the galaxy, that everything would go peachy and according to her plans.

"And what if you need protection from him?" he asked, cocking an eyebrow.

She looked confused. "What?"

"Not everyone is an upstanding citizen. I'm sure you know of people who have been abused by their spouses."

"Of course," she said, sounding defensive. "I'm not naive." Ram had a few things to say about *that*, but he decided to keep them to himself for now. "But Tennel isn't like that. He would never—"

"Yeah, 'cause it sounds like you know him so well."

Carina let out a long sigh, and Ram could see the fight draining from her. "Ram, why are we doing this?"

"I already told you — I think everyone should have some basic defense training. Now get your butt on the mat, and start stretching." He grinned at her. "Besides, you can always show off your skills to your husband in the bedroom."

She scowled and blushed a deep red — he loved when she managed to do both at the same time. Another tidbit he wasn't ever going to reveal to her.

"Ugh, you're such a barbarian. I'm not doing this. If I really need to defend myself, I'll just run away."

"Yeah, because that's worked out so well for you before." Her scowl deepened. She really was grumpy this morning. "You want to test that?" He slowly pushed himself to his feet and raised an eyebrow.

She looked at him incredulously, then narrowed her eyes and took a step back. He grinned and mirrored her moment. She stepped back again, and he followed with another step. It seemed to click for her that he was serious. The hint of a smile played on her lips, and then she turned and fled.

He let out a small chuckle before he took off after her. She made it almost to the hatchway of the training room, mostly because he didn't push himself to catch up sooner.

He leaned in as he caught up and wrapped an arm around her midsection while coming to a halt. She let out a sound of protest, but he used the last of his forward momentum to wrap a leg around hers and knocked her off balance. It was much more gentle than when he had first chased her, but it brought her down to the mat nonetheless.

Her hands ineffectually pried at his arm that was still holding her, and he forced her down in one, abrupt movement, enough to pin her to the training mat, but keeping his full weight off of her. She jerked against him, and he could feel the rapid beat of her heart.

"*This*," he said, looking her straight in the eye. "This is why you need to know how to defend yourself. So you at least have a fighting chance if someone *ever* tries to go after you."

She gritted her teeth. "The only one who's ever gone after me like this is you. Both times!" She let her head thunk down on the mat as she sighed, finally ceasing her struggles. "You've made your point, though."

He pushed up off of her and helped her to her feet. Then he led her back over to the training area he'd reserved for the morning.

"We'll start with the basics," he told her, after he had guided her through his normal warm-up routine. "Hands here," he said as he firmly gripped her wrists and moved them into position. "Keep your stance loose." He nudged one of her ankles with the toe of his boot.

"What does that even mean?" she asked, looking up at him skeptically.

"The worst thing in a fight is for your enemy to be able to know exactly where you will be when they decide to strike. Being loose means fluid, able to move when you see the sign of that strike. Even if you're not able to get completely out of the way, you can block or deflect. There are times to be tight too, but only if you need to protect vital parts from blows."

She made a face, clearly unsure of how to put it into practice.

"It's a bit of a feel thing," he admitted. "It takes some time, but you'll learn it. Start like this." He took his stance, and she followed. He moved her a little more into the true stance until he was pleased — trying not to let his hands linger, but enjoying her closeness all the same.

"Now, again, it's a feel, but keep your arms loose, ready to move — your ankles and knees ready to move wherever you can," he said, demonstrating how she should have her limbs ready. Once he was satisfied she at least understood the concept, he continued. "If you're attacked, the element of surprise is your best advantage," he said. "They'll likely underestimate you, so you need to strike fast and haul stars out of there."

Carina frowned. "I thought all this was so you could show me to fight."

"First, I'm going to teach you basic defense," he amended. "You're not going to win a brawl — not without a lot more training. I'm going to teach you a few things that will help you actually get away if you're ever in a dangerous situation. So we'll start with this, and go from there."

"Got it," she said, nodding. "And it's not like I'm going to be around here much longer anyway."

"Mmm," he said, noncommittal. That was a can of spaceworms he did not want to get into right now. The whole diplomacy talks had been so rocky they could use them to build a bridge across the Askelan Ocean.

"Have you heard anything about how the negotiations are going?" she asked, tilting her head so she could look up at him. He saw the hope on her face, and it felt like a punch to the gut.

"Tell you what," he said, ignoring the pit in his stomach. "Do a good job this morning, and I'll tell you what I know." He knew he shouldn't have said that, but the words just came out. It was a bad idea. How could he explain in a way that didn't crush her hopes?

But she lit up instantly, and he saw the determination in her eyes. "Well, then, what are we waiting for?"

The look on her face both pained him — he didn't like deceiving her — and filled him with a warmth that tempered his hesitations. He didn't want to risk having her fade away on him again. She looked so alive standing there, hopeful and eager. He forced himself to smile.

Ram took her through a crash course of basic defense, and she stayed intensely focused — her reluctance from earlier evaporated. It was obvious she had zero experience, but she made a good effort to absorb what he was teaching. Her enthusiasm was refreshing, and soon any hesitations he had were far from his mind.

He managed to somehow make her laugh so hard, she'd fallen to the floor with tears in her eyes, after telling her the name of a particular move. He'd watched in bafflement — apparently it was a Seuturan cultural euphemism he hadn't known about — and in wonder at how her face transformed when she laughed. He wished he could do it more often, then immediately chastised himself for that thought. Thinking of ways to make his captive laugh should not be something occupying his mind. Besides, he had no idea how much longer he had with her.

"Good job," he told her as she successfully completed a series of defensive jabs at vital parts on him. He wore special padding for the fight, but she had done well with her motions. His compliment seemed to make her overconfident and she took a step towards him for another jab. It left her completely vulnerable. He easily flipped her to the mat, coming down gently on top of her.

She tried to scowl, but was still half smiling. She was still panting slightly from the exertions of the training, and her braid was partially askew, and damp with sweat. This close, he could smell her — like tsyr flowers and sunshine. He reached and adjusted a few loose strands of hair, brushing them off her face. She looked up at him curiously. They were quiet a long moment — just looking at one another, the cares of the galaxy far away. And it almost made him wish for impossible things.

The spell was broken when someone across the room knocked a training dummy over, and the loud clang echoed throughout the training room. Carina blinked and cleared her throat. She squirmed beneath him.

"I did your silly training," she said, face suddenly serious. "You promised to tell me what you know."

"Of course, Buttercup," he said, pushing to his feet. He helped her up.

"Well?" she said, her playful attitude from earlier gone. It was a good dose of reality for him — and he was irritated he'd even fallen under her blasted spell. He needed to keep his head on straight.

"Sounds like they've overcome a major hurdle in the negotiations," Ram said. "There should be a resolution soon." Overly simplified, perhaps, but it was all she needed to know for now.

Her face lit up with excitement. "Really? So, do you know when I can go home?"

Ram frowned. "How am I supposed to know that, woman? It's not like I'm sitting in on the blasted diplomacy meetings."

She let out a short, happy laugh, then reached over, giving him a brief hug, stunning him. She headed off toward the locker room, and he could swear he heard her humming quietly. He stood there in dazed silence for a long moment.

"Man," Feingo said as he came up beside him, laying an arm on his shoulder and leaning into him. "You're in trouble."

Ram grunted. Not if he could help it. He just had to keep himself steady, and keep his focus on their mission. "Not as much trouble as you'll be in when I wipe the deck with your face."

Feingo let out a chuckle. "Dunno, seems like you might be worn out after all that this morning."

Ram cursed and grabbed Feingo's arm before he could move it. He twisted and tossed him to the mat. As he walked away to get a drink of water before his real training began, he heard Feingo still laughing quietly on the floor.

Chapter 16

It was five days later when Ram took Carina to visit the small group of women prisoners again, which put her in even higher spirits than she was before. She was hopeful that they might not even need to go through with their escape plans if the negotiations were concluded soon.

When she arrived, Ram took the same position at the window, a stoic look on his face. Yeunay was resting this afternoon, but the rest of the women Carina had met a couple weeks ago were sitting together on one of the cushioned couches. Kimura waved her over as soon as she spotted her. They were all reading from small, hand-held tablets except Niki. Niki seemed to be lost in her own thoughts, sitting beside Shaian, almost as if hiding in her shadow. Triska barely looked up from her tablet as Carina sat down, but did pause to give a warm smile. Shaian had been reading hers with a stern look, as if her expression alone could render what she read as false. She lowered hers as she saw Carina.

"I have to admit, their culture is interesting," Kimura said, setting her tablet down on the table in front of them. "They've just recently united as a planet. It's incredible what they can do in such a short time."

"Ram mentioned they were split just a few decades ago." Carina said. "I wonder if he would let me get a tablet like that."

Even once the words were out of her mouth, they felt silly to her. She wouldn't be here nearly long enough to enjoy it.

"They're uncultured brutes," Shaian said, setting her tablet down as well. "We don't know if what they put in these is true, but even if half of it is, they lived in paradise and spent centuries bickering about it instead of making something from it. And when they finally did, they used it to attack us."

"I thought them taking us as hostages was some sort of retaliation," Carina said.

"Of course that's what they would say," Shaian said, scoffing. "But retaliation for *what*? And against whom? Seutura? Why would we have bothered attacking them in the first place? How could we have?"

"They do seem to have some advanced technology."

"And who knows how they acquired it," Shaian retorted. "Or the lives they sacrificed to get it."

Carina had no reply to that. She had seen her share of deaths in the mines. Sacrifices to advance Seutura, but then again Seutura was a harsher planet than Varus seemed to be, so she wasn't sure if they could be compared.

"Another group of prisoners were assigned keepers," Niki said quietly in the silence that followed. A note of fear permeated her voice. Carina realized she genuinely thought the Varusians were that scary. The way she sat, it was as if she thought Shaian's presence could protect her.

"It's not too bad," Carina heard herself saying, with a strange desire to defend Ram's character. On the battlefield he would be terrifying, but he'd been kind to her. She was still a prisoner, no doubt about it, but she felt strangely safe with him around. That thought actually made her feel miffed. He was her captor after all. *So why am I defending him then?* But for some reason she kept talking, trying to convince Niki they all weren't bad. "I mostly just help

Ram with his duties. I feel more like I'm being forced to do chores than being treated like a captive."

"Hopefully not much for much longer," Shaian said, glancing toward the windows. "We've made some progress on the escape plan." Her eyes flicked around the room as if she expected a Varusian soldier to pop out from nowhere.

"But...Ram told me the negotiations were going well, and should be coming to an end soon," Carina said, giving a reassuring smile. "We might not even need to escape."

Shaian gave her a patient look. "*Ram* said? Do you think it's wise to count on that?"

Carina gave a small sigh, and shook her head. Probably not, she knew. Maybe it was wishful thinking that things would turn out fine. Or maybe she didn't like the idea of Ram lying to her. In any case, it wouldn't hurt to have a backup plan.

"We've figured out a way to get through the zero-g tunnel without a Varusian soldier," Shaian continued. "It's slow though. Escaping here is the easy part though. The biggest problem we're still trying to figure out is transport. The main hangar bay holds all the transport ships, but it's heavily guarded. There's another bay that holds starfighters, but it's equally guard, and the fighters are only single-person craft." Shaian looked around and spoke even quieter. "One of the guys managed to smuggle a weapon."

"A weapon?" Carina said, growing tense. "But we aren't going to hurt anyone, right?"

Shaian sighed. "None of us *wants* to hurt anyone. But we are prisoners of war. And there's no telling what will happen, negotiations or not."

"But Ram—"

"Carina," Shaian interrupted, giving her a patient look. "Don't you think you're becoming a little...attached?"

"To Ram?" she asked, her voice suddenly dry. It was a preposterous idea. "Of course not! If it weren't for him, I wouldn't even be in this mess. And he's infuriating, and... and..."

"Oh, yeah," Triska said dryly, looking up from her tablet. "She's attached all right." She leaned back with a smirk and a toss of her red hair, seeming to get a strange amusement from the situation.

"I'm not attached!" Her voice was louder than she had expected. Several women from other tables looked over at them, which made Carina blush. She lowered her voice and spoke again. "I just — I'm trying to be content and patient, and...he hasn't been completely awful."

"Mmmhmm. Tell you what — if *you* don't want to be attached to him, I'll volunteer," Triska said. Carina rolled her eyes, annoyance rising up in her.

"Just remember to keep your head on straight," Shaian said, ignoring Triska. "If you'd rather not be involved, that's fine. You out there have the best chance, but we can only get so many out."

"I want to be involved," Carina said firmly. "I want to go home." Shaian regarded her face assessingly, and nodded.

After that the conversation shifted from the escape to more mundane things. How others thought of their conditions in the section. Thoughts on the barbaric Varusian culture. Carina let it be. It could be that plans were still being decided, or that they didn't fully trust her yet. In either case, as long as they took her along she was fine with it. Her thoughts drifted to Bryn.

"Have you been able to find out anything about my friend, Bryn?" Carina asked.

"Nothing," Shaian said. "That doesn't mean much, however. Occasionally they move some of us from one section to another, but it's unpredictable. If she's in another section we may never know."

"Do all the sections know about the escape?" Carina asked, braving back into the topic it seemed they were trying to avoid.

Shaian shook her head. "No. We're being careful, like you have to be in any conspiracy. To be honest, I only told you because Yeunay vouched for you, and you're out there and we can use any help we can get. If we can, we will let as many people know right before we leave, but even then we have to be careful that no one will inform on us."

"No one would do that, would they?" Carina said, taken back. "Turn on fellow Seuturans?"

"There are always some. They could even justify it as doing the right thing. Not wanting us to die in the escape. Thinking Varus will be better for all of us." Carina couldn't help notice Shaian's glance at Triska, but the latter was engrossed again in her tablet. "Some of them may still let us try, but others will think they are doing us a favor by reporting us."

The conversation died back down at that point. Talk picked up again about people and things Carina didn't know and hardly cared about, compared to the thought of escape or the possibility of her friend being here and her not knowing it. It was almost a relief when Ram came and told her that her time was up.

Afterwards, as Ram led her back to her quarters, he glanced over and gave her an odd look. "What were you ladies whispering about?"

Carina blanched, terror filling her. She tried to think of what to say. Had he somehow caught wind of their escape plan? Had he let her go back in hopes of finding out details about it and interrogating her? She looked at him, and saw his face was just genuinely curious. Still, she had to be careful not to give him anything to be suspicious about.

"Nothing," she asid, wincing when her voice almost came out like a squeak.

Ram raised an eyebrow. Definitely his *I'm not buying it face*. She thought quickly. "Uh, one of the other women thinks…you're attractive." Carina flushed.

"Who? The one with short, blonde hair?"

"No, uh Triska. Red hair."

"Huh," Ram said, looking thoughtfully back at the corridor in front of them. "Interesting."

Carina frowned, wondering what *that* was supposed to mean. Something that felt suspiciously like a pang of jealousy sprang up in her. She squashed it back down.

"She's not your type," Carina said, staring straight ahead. It was concern for Triska that made Carina speak. At least that's what she told herself. Triska would be far too susceptible if Ram showed interest in her. It wouldn't be good for her.

"Oh, really?" Ram asked with a chuckle. "As if you know my type."

"Airheaded and easily impressed?" she asked sweetly.

Ram snorted. "How about docile, sweet, and does as they're told?"

Carina made a disgusted sound. "You are a barbarian."

Ram grinned. "Bet I can guess your type."

"Dependable. Steady. Nice."

Ram laughed loudly. "Oh, that's what you think you want. Boring. But not what you need."

"What do you know about what I need?" Carina said, stopping abruptly in the hallway with her hands on her hips, and nearly causing someone in a dark blue uniform to crash into her. Ram scowled and pulled her off to the side of the corridor.

"Sure as stars not some imbecile who's just marrying you for a bigger housing allotment."

"I'm marrying him for the same reasons," she said. "And I like *boring*. I want *boring*."

He leaned in close, an infuriating smirk on his lips. "I bet after you go home to your quiet, doldrum life, and marry that boring little husband, it won't take long before you're restless and discontent. You've had a taste of adventure, Buttercup. And deny it all you want, but you like it."

*   *   *

Carina remained irritated with Ram for the rest of the day, but it took more effort to stay that way than she expected. Ram didn't apologize, but he did get her an extra spiced roll that night for dinner, and took her to the small on-board garden again the next morning since it was his day off. After that, it was difficult to stay upset with him. It really was her favorite place on board. And by the end of their time there, she was reluctantly laughing at his absurd jokes, and listening in awe to his tales of the wonders of Varus.

Unfortunately he cut it off just after telling her about something called a rainforest, which was just as unbelievable as it sounded — enough rain and warmth to make the surface more green than brown. She wanted him to tell her more about the plants and wildlife there, but he said he had to be somewhere that evening and that she couldn't come. She was mildly annoyed that she was forced to stay in her room. But at least he left her an extra serving of chocolate mousse and a tablet to read from. She curled up in the chair in her room with the lights softened, and read more about the rainforest he spoke of. A place that seemed almost beyond imagining.

Chapter 17

"At ease soldier," a voice said as Ram entered the quarters.

The room wasn't particularly big, as ship space was a premium on the *Architeuthis*, but the living space was still larger than the three small rooms Ram and Carina shared for their quarters. He had only been in here once this voyage, but he recognized many of Halvar's effects. Two old swords, as different from each other as night and day and not nearly up to modern military standards, stood on a rack. A map of a small town that only those who knew their warfare would recognize as important, marked up with the battle movements of one key day. A few books, now outdated by tablets, stacked on the shelves.

Halvar himself sat in his off duty slacks, leaning forward in a chair with his arms resting on the tabletop. Thekla, also in off duty attire, was sitting in a second chair. Both held a drink in their hands. A third chair completed the circle, empty and waiting for him.

"Is this an ambush, sir?" Ram asked, looking at Halvar. He couldn't quite get himself to relax. Not with how Halvar and Thekla looked far too calm. That meant they were of one mind about something, and Ram had long ago learned just how dangerous that could be.

"Come off it, Ram," Thekla said in his low growl. Even sitting back in the chair with the drink in his hand he could not be mistaken for anything but a soldier. He'd been known to scare new recruits just by looking at them.

Of course, the jagged scar on the side of his face could probably intimidate most men without any help from the rest of him. He looked entirely too self assured sitting there for Ram comfort.

"Come on, sit down Ram," Halvar said, standing up and ushering Ram over to the empty chair. "It's not an ambush. I wouldn't do that to you. It's just, well…"

"A surprise attack against an unprepared target?" Ram asked. A thought crept into his mind and lodged in his throat. He knew exactly where this was going. Still, Ram found himself sitting in the empty seat, propelled there by the force of Halvar's personality and Thekla's unyielding determination. Ram had been in his share of battles where he had relied on both of those. In the heat of combat either of them, by force of will, seemed to be able to get the Moirae to look the right way when all hope seemed lost. Ram owed much to both of these men. The fact that they owed him back didn't diminish that.

"It's not like that, Ram," Thekla said, taking a sip from his glass.

"Then what is it like?" Ram asked. He found a drink had ended up in his own hand. He sighed and took a sip.

"Do you remember what we said at Kelton?" Halvar asked.

Ram nodded. Of course he remembered. It was the first place he saw Halvar command. A barely tried officer turning the tide of battle, humiliating the other officer in command, Mikael, in the process. Ram and a much better-looking Thekla ended up by his side by mere chance, but stayed there until the end.

"We'd have each other's backs, both on and off the battlefield," Ram said.

"You need to get your head together," Thekla said, sitting forward and pointing. "It's gotten so bad that a thousand laps wouldn't get it out of the clouds."

"I'm fine," Ram said forcefully.

Thekla gave Halvar a look. It was an *I-told-you-so look*.

"Your prisoner," Halvar started. "Carina Mosaido, right?"

"She's been behaving," Ram said, feeling suddenly defensive.

Thekla snorted. "If demanding tea and cookies, and evenings spent at the star observatory is behaving."

"I've been making sure she's been doing her fair share of work, and has been integrated into the crew as well as possible for a zero-clearance status." He plunked the glass down on the table.

"Ram, the integration was meant to help ease some of these captives' fears, as well as give them a bit of insight into Varusian culture," Halvar said. "I was against the decision to take civilian captives as well as military, but I was outvoted. I backed the integration as a way to ease them."

"I know, sir," Ram said. He took another drink. Halvar was a man Ram would follow into the Abyss — both because he knew Halvar wouldn't march into the Abyss without good reason and because he knew the Abyss had a good chance of ending up on the losing side. After all, Kelton had essentially been that. Thekla must have been thinking the same thing because at that moment he scratched his face around his scar.

"My point is that integration is about assuaging their fears, not getting attached to them."

Ram sighed. He would rather face a hundred Cortese soldiers than be here right now. But part of him knew they were right. He did enjoy his time with Carina, but he wasn't going to get too attached.

"It's not like she's going to be here long," Ram said. "I know there've been a hiccup in negotiations, but they're bound to get past it. Seutura wants their citizens back, I'm sure."

"What's the last you heard about the talks?" Halvar asked, swirling his drink around in his cup.

"Outright denial of the attack. I heard we gave them our records to show what happened."

"We did, but then they threatened to cut off talks."

"Even with all our hostages?"

"They said they wouldn't negotiate over the hostages. We're going to call their bluff."

"And if it's not a bluff?" Ram asked, a pit lodging in his stomach.

"We'll know soon enough," Halvar said. "If they don't reinstate talks, we will take action soon." He gave Ram a warning look. "There are some in command who have suggested we execute some hostages to send a message."

Ram felt his blood run cold, and his hand tightened around his glass. Mikael most likely, and others who followed him. There'd been a constant power play between Halvar and Mikael for as long as he'd known them. "That's idiotic."

Halvar snorted, taking another sip. "There's plenty in command eager for blood. Don't forget what brought us here."

Like Ram needed that reminder. He was one of the first to cry for blood. But this was different. Carina was…

He sat there, struck by his self-realization. She was a Seuturan after all. The enemy. His attachments to her didn't change that.

Outwardly he grimaced. Thekla noticed and leaned forward. He pointed at Ram with the hand still holding the glass.

"And that is why this silly attachment is going to end you up in more trouble than a skee in a cor pond," he growled.

Chapter 18

Carina stared out at the stars as she sat on the cool floor of the star observatory in a pleasant trance as Ram deftly braided her hair. It was a strange realization that the big soldier could do such a thing. She had complained about her hair that morning, and somehow that had resulted with a trip to the observatory and him working on her hair later in the afternoon after their tasks were done. She closed her eyes for a moment, enjoying the gentle tugs and smooth movements of her hair.

"You're really good at this," she murmured.

"Mmm," Ram responded distantly. "Sisters."

"I didn't know you had sisters," she said, opening her eyes. "How many? Are they older or younger?"

He was quiet for a long moment. "Two. Both younger."

"Are they on board?" She knew it was an absurd question once she asked. It was a military vessel. The odds of them being in the military and on board were next to nothing.

"No," he said after another moment of hesitation.

She was about to tease him about his taciturn responses, when something rumbled through the ship. It was subtle, but she could feel the vibrations through the floor. She couldn't remember feeling anything like it since she'd been on board.

"What was that?"

"Hmm?" Ram sounded as though she'd startled him from his thoughts.

"Didn't you feel that? That rumble."

"Mmm," he said, continuing to weave her hair. "Think I heard something about a new orbit pattern."

Carina felt a surge of excitement. "Does this have to do with the negotiations? Are they — Why didn't you tell me?" She felt exasperated. Of course he hadn't thought to tell her. She'd tried to restrain her questions recently — knowing it was going to take time, and having been assured that at least the escape plan was somewhat in motion.

"Calm yourself," Ram growled out, as he maneuvered the last few strands of her hair. He was quiet as he finished and tied off the second braid. She turned and looked up at him expectantly, trying to keep her excitement contained.

Ram looked down at her, expression unreadable. Finally, he said, "Yes, it has to do with the talks. I didn't want to tell you anything until things were finalized."

She grinned. She was going to go home.

*   *   *

Carina was cleaning Ram's armor in the locker room, enjoying the peace and muted noise echoing in from the training room. Ram was still out there, helping someone clean up after a training exercise in the other room. He'd sent her ahead because it was running long.

She was still practically humming with excitement from her conversation with Ram the day before. *Finally.* After nearly six weeks of captivity, she would get to go home and put this nightmare behind her. She couldn't wait to have solid ground under her feet, see the sun, and breathe fresh, cold air. Her plants were no doubt dead. But if Tennel wanted to get married soon, and they were approved for the transfer, then perhaps there would be a little spare income to buy more seedlings. She could cook again.

She ignored the part of her that said she'd miss life here. That was ridiculous. She couldn't possibly miss life as a prisoner.

Carina was musing and daydreaming of home when she heard the stomp of boots and laughter at the entrance of the locker room, out of sight where she was cleaning Ram's armor by his locker.

"What's your assignment for this afternoon?" one voice asked.

"Ah, gotta help wrap up repairs on the *Rhincodon*. Nearly there, then they're going to get it moved back to the main bay in a few days," the second said. She didn't immediately recognize the voices, so they must be from another squad.

"Thank the stars we finally get to head home," the first said, and she immediately perked up. Of course they would be going home after they dropped off the captives. Perhaps she'd overhear when they would be able to transport the prisoners back to Seutura. She gripped the armor in her hand, heart pounding with excitement.

"I know. Thankfully we're still in the window where the trip home won't be too long."

"Yeah. Been thinking about putting in a request for a captive," the first voice said.

And with that, it felt as though the gravity had been turned off, and all the air sucked right out. She froze.

"Wasn't sure I wanted to, but now that we know they're coming with us for sure, might as well get someone to have a little extra help at home."

The other soldier chuckled. "No surprise the talks went south. I can't believe we were even trying to negotiate with the Seuturans."

They continued to speak, but everything faded away, and all she could hear was the rush of blood and thudding of her heart.

She wasn't going home.

Her heart felt as though it was going to shatter.

Ram.

He had to have known. The ugly truth hit her. He had been lying to her. Had he been lying from the start or just recently, she wondered. Did it matter? All the placating, saying just the right things to keep her hoping, keep her appeased. And she'd fallen for it. Never questioned it. How could she have been so foolish?

"Buttercup?"

She looked up, startled at the sound.

Chapter 19

Ram came into the locker room, feeling more enthused than he had in a while. Training had gone well this morning, the men extra invigorated.

"Buttercup?" he called out again. "You done? Don't know about you, but I'm starving." He came around the row of armor lockers. The grin fell off his face as soon as he saw her — ashen face, eyes unfocused. "What's up, Buttercup? You okay?"

"You knew." Her voice was weak, and it took a second for her words to penetrate his mind as he strode through the locker room.

Damn. He drew up short. He had hoped to break the news to her gently. Someone must have blabbed. And he was going to give them a good thrashing when he found out who.

"Buttercup—" he started to say.

"Don't call me that, you lying scum!" She shoved the armor off the bench, eyes blazing and breaths coming in short pants. "When were you going to tell me? How long did you plan on stringing my hopes along?" He winced, and she let out an incredulous laugh. "I can't believe I was so stupid."

It wasn't as though he'd wanted to lie to her. He just had no idea how to break the news to her without crushing her. She'd finally started to seem happy.

"Carina," he said, starting to approach slowly.

She glared back at him, fists clenched. "Were you just going to wait until we got back to Varus? Say, 'Surprise! You're stuck here forever!'"

He stopped a meter from her and scowled, anger flaring. "Of course not!" he snapped. *Stuck.* Of course she would view it that way. He'd been naive to think otherwise. That she might learn to enjoy a bit of adventure.

"You *are* a barbarian," she said, her voice low and fierce. But it was the sorrow in her face that really cut into him. "You and all the other Varusians. Got bored conquering each other, and decided to set your greedy sights on whatever else you could find."

Ram's eyes narrowed. Any compassion he held evaporated in that moment — burning anger and his own sorrow replacing it in a flash. "*We're* barbarians?" he asked, jaw clenching. "We're not the ones who wiped out an entire research facility and murdered hundreds of innocent people."

Carina jerked back, her eyes going wide. "What? What are you talking about?"

Ram's chest tightened. The wave of sorrow became almost overwhelming. He glanced around the locker room, stiffening. "We don't need to do this here."

"Oh, yes, there it is again. Deflection." Carina scoffed.

Ram snapped his eyes back to her, scowling. "And what in the stars is that supposed to mean?"

"It's what you've been doing this whole time I've been here! Every question, anything going on — deflect, deflect, distract. The tea, the garden, the observatory — everything. Just keep the prisoner appeased, and she'll be nice and docile." Carina looked disgusted. "And idiot that I am, I was completely blind to it."

His anger rose — at her, at all of them, at himself.

Of course she didn't understand. And he'd been the fool, thinking he could befriend the enemy. For thinking a Seuturan could understand what he was going through.

He stepped forward, and Carina flinched back away from him, hitting the locker behind her. He saw fear and wariness in her eyes, and for once he didn't care. He grabbed her arm, hauling her toward the exit, ignoring the pile of armor on the floor and her protests.

People quickly cleared a path ahead of them as he walked away from the training area and back toward his quarters. Carina came reluctantly, and tried — albeit feebly — to protest.

By the time they reached his quarters, his rage had gone from an inferno to a low simmer. All the power was still behind it, but controlled, focused into a flame that could cut through hardened vizsteel. Carina was wide-eyed and breathless as he keyed the hatch closed, but she stood her ground. Even when he turned to face her, she only took a small step back, arms crossed in front of her.

"What did you mean about innocent people?" she asked, eyes wary.

Ram took a deep breath. "Eight months ago our research center on Uatera was attacked, and all eight-hundred and twelve of its inhabitants killed. We found that most were killed *after* they had surrendered. Slaughtered without a care."

Carina's eyes widened in shock. "That's...awful." Her brow furrowed. "But what does that have to do with us?"

Ram stared at her. "That was the attack. It was carried out by Seutura."

"That's impossible," Carina said, shaking her head. "Besides a couple small research centers of our own, we don't even care about off-planet matters. We have enough to worry about on our own world."

"There's no mistake," Ram said, walking over to the viewing screen on the wall and staring at the moving photos on it.

"But, I'm sure if they just talked—"

"What do you think they've been blasted doing in the negotiations the past six weeks?"

Carina watched him carefully, still pressed up close to the wall, arms crossed in front of her as though to protect herself. "So that's the leverage we were taken for," she said slowly.

"Taken as leverage, and for retaliation," Ram confirmed.

"But—" Carina frowned. "The talks didn't go well? Did...did they not fight to get us back?" Ram felt a twinge of sympathy at the confusion and sorrow on her face, but he suppressed it.

"There were complications."

"What complications?"

Ram growled. "How about your government denying everything in the face of the evidence for starters?"

Carina was quiet for a long moment. Then she hesitantly said, "Ram, I'm sorry about your people. But that doesn't justify taking people captive, especially if—"

He turned to her, his anger flaring up again. "Doesn't it? A life for a life."

"But none of us — none of the captives — did anything wrong."

"Neither did the eight-hundred twelve people in that facility." Ram closed his eyes. "Mircea, my sweet sister, was one of the geologists in the facility. She lived there with her husband and their child. You know I helped her get the post? She worked so hard for it, and a friend of mine was able to push her application along. Do you know how excited she was when she got accepted?"

The emotional pain cut into him like a knife. It hurt just as bad as the day he'd received the comm transmission that delivered the news. Worse, even. That first day, that first week, had just been numbness. A sense of surreal disbelief. The grief had morphed into something even more painful. He had continually repressed it — fought it back with the utter focus on his mission. Appeased it with the intoxicating thought of revenge. Seuturans had taken his sister and his sweet nephew. How gloriously good it felt to take something away from them. To bring them a sort of loss that would make them understand his same grief and pain.

A gentle hand on his arm made his eyes snap open, and he found himself gazing into the deep, blue depths of Carina's eyes, filled with compassion. It fueled his anger.

And reignited the uncomfortable stirrings of guilt.

He shook her off.

"Ram..."

"Get in your quarters. I have some things to take care of." She looked as though she was about to say something else. "Go!" he snapped.

She turned and walked over to the hatch to her room. She hesitated in the hatchway, and glanced back over her shoulder at him. "I'm so sorry, Ram," she said softly, then disappeared into her room.

He stalked over and slammed his fist on the keypad, then keyed the lock. Sorry wouldn't bring back those who were lost.

Neither would keeping a prisoner of war, a voice in the back of his head whispered. He ignored it. She might not deserve it, but neither did his sister. They had to do something to balance the scales.

Chapter 20

Carina sat, numb, in the chair in her room. She'd heard Ram key the lock on her door — something he hadn't done in weeks.

Her mind was a tumultuous sea, and she felt lost and buffeted. Sorrow and rage mixed in a typhoon so large she felt as though she might drown in.

Sorrow for Ram. To lose part of his family like that. She just couldn't believe her planet had been involved in something so awful. She couldn't imagine the grief he must feel.

Rage at Ram for hiding the truth from her.

She wasn't going home. She would *never* be going home.

She had just been a pawn in a larger conflict. A war. There really was a war. It hadn't felt real this whole time. She'd convinced herself that it was all a misunderstanding — that surely, if they sat down and talked through it, everything would get sorted out. How naive she'd been.

She cursed the implacable, unreasonableness of the Varusians. And she cursed her own planet for not fighting harder for their own people. Had they even tried to get them back? Or were they just chalked up to be unfortunate casualties of war? Written off — better to be sacrificed to the Varusians to appease them, rather than risk angering them further and putting Seutura in danger.

Then the flood of tears came. She was to be a captive forever, a prisoner — on a strange planet, in a strange society. Given to a man who hated her people. Never to be her own person again.

She sobbed, grieving for her loss — her dreams of a quiet life. Of growing her herbs, cooking, marrying a steady, stable man. She would never have any of it. It felt like all her hope was being sucked away, as though into the infinite blackness of space.

Carina straightened, angrily wiping at her face. This didn't mean their escape plan couldn't go through. There was still a chance, if they could get off the *Architeuthis* soon enough, before it had a chance to significantly accelerate toward Varus.

But they still needed a way off the ship.

Then it came to her — a piece of fuel to feed her spark of hope. She suddenly knew how they might do it.

Chapter 21

The upper command room of the *Architeuthis* was a place for formal meetings and discussions. It was primarily for the officers, which was why Ram was surprised when he received a summons to go there.

It was late at night. Ram was technically off duty, and getting called in put him in an even fouler mood than he'd been in before. He had been having doubts about his treatment of Carina. He knew she didn't deserve this, but what could he do now? They were both stuck with their fates.

His mood dived several more notches when he stepped into the command room. Mikael stood at the holo table, fully uniformed and examining what looked like a map of a province of Seutura. No one else was present.

"Corporal, thank you for joining me," Mikael said, stepping back from the table.

"What do you want?" Ram asked. He didn't even bother saluting. He could be punished for that, but he was tired. It had been an exhausting, emotional day. He wanted to sleep it away, and dredge up the energy to face tomorrow.

"I've heard some disconcerting news. It seems someone is getting a little attached to his captive," Mikael said, raising an eyebrow. Ram clenched his fists, envisioning pummel Mikael on the floor.

"Is that what this is about, Mikael? Petty jealousy?" Ram shook his head mockingly. "I thought even scum like you would be above that."

Mikael straightened, and Ram saw a dangerous glint enter his eye. It didn't frighten him — he could beat Mikael in a fight easily. But the ramifications for assaulting a superior officer weren't insignificant.

"I'd urge you to take this seriously," Mikael said, his voice soft. "We are the vanguard of this war. Our actions will dictate how those who follow us will act. We must show true loyalty to Varus."

"And that's why you advocated taking civilian prisoners? To show loyalty?" Ram asked.

"Military prisoners are just that — military," Mikael said dismissively. "Expendable. Those are the people who are expected to die in a war. Civilians were killed in the attack against us. So why should we care about the inconvenience of Seuturan civilians?"

Ram had nothing to say about that. He had all but said the same thing to Carina earlier.

"When Halvar wanted to integrate some of the prisoners, I was against it, but I eventually saw some value to it. Our people could finally see the Seuturan's true natures. But there's been some hiccups. There have been whispers of some soldiers becoming compromised..." Mikael trailed off, giving a little shrug.

"I'm loyal to Varus," Ram said, keeping his voice steady. Losing his temper with Mikael would only give him fuel, and might risk having Carina taken away. "I thought the point of the integration was to show Seuturan captives our society, especially if the negotiations didn't go as planned."

"Yes, of course," Mikael said. "But not to the point where they have too much sway over us, or potentially access valuable intel or technology."

"I understand."

Mikael smirked. "They're little more than slaves, you know. That's what they will be back on Varus, once we arrive."

Ram took a slow, steadying breath. Mikael was just trying to get a rise out of him. And he'd win if he did.

"I haven't found one that struck my fancy yet," Mikael continued, running his fingers along the conference table. "Well—" he looked up at Ram "—other than that little beauty of yours. If you ever tire of her, *or* I find any evidence that you are compromised, I'd be more than happy to take her off your hands."

Dead. Mikael should be dead. Shot out an airlock. Or better yet, slowly tortured, and then put in an airlock with a slow leak. And Ram needed to get out of here before the temptation to do so became too great.

"Am I dismissed?"

"Of course, Corporal," Mikael said.

Ram turned on his heel and left the room, forcing himself to take even steps.

Thekla was waiting just outside the door, leaning against the bulkhead, arms crossed. He pushed off from the wall when Ram stepped out. The hatch slid shut and Thekla gave him an appraising look. "You look like you need to pummel something."

Ram grunted and began striding down the corridor. "The only thing I need to pummel is Mikael."

"That's a good way to get yourself court-martialed," Thekla said, falling into step beside him.

"Maybe it's worth it."

"I take it the meeting went well then. This about your girl?"

Ram remained silent, clenching his fists. Of course it was about her. He felt like *everything* recently had become about her, down to the air he breathed. "Mikael threatened to have her taken if there's any suggestion I've become too attached and may be compromising Varus' security," Ram managed to get out.

Thekla huffed. He didn't say anything, but he didn't need to. The conversation with Thekla and Halvar came back unbidden.

"So you agree with him?" Ram said accusingly.

"I don't think you'd do anything purposefully to compromise Varus," Thekla said, giving him a level look. "But all Mikael needs is enough to bring a case against you. And between him and Kasperi, with the sway they have in upper command, that wouldn't be difficult."

Ram forced his breaths to stay even. Captain Kasperi was similarly minded to Mikael and could cause him trouble, but Mikael was his main concern right now. He'd murder Mikael before he ever let him get his hands on Carina, court martial be damned.

"What are you saying?" he asked Thekla, keeping his eyes locked on the corridor in front of them.

"Just what we said before. Watch your step, at least until we get back to Varus. Keep your distance." Thekla looked over at him pointedly. "Don't be teaching her combat techniques and getting mushy in the training room."

Ram started to object. Basic self-defense was hardly combat techniques, and everyone should be able to defend themselves. And they hadn't *gotten mushy*.

Thekla held up a hand. "Honestly, I don't know what's going on between you two, and frankly I don't give a crap as long as you're not letting yourself lag as a soldier. But obviously word got back to Mikael, and he'll use any solid evidence against you. This isn't just about you, Ram. You know that. Mikael is trying to use you to get at Halvar. You do something stupid, and the repercussions will weaken Halvar's standing. Just pull back and keep some perspective." He shook his head. "It's not like there's a reasonable future with this girl, Ram. She's a Seuturan."

Thekla left, leaving Ram to walk alone back to his quarters. He was right, of course, about Mikael. It wasn't Ram he was really going after. Ram was just a pawn in this.

But pawn or not, he knew Mikael would follow through on his threat, as much a power play to undermine Halvar as to get something he wanted. But Ram wouldn't let them take Carrina away. He just wasn't sure what in the stars he was going to do.

Chapter 22

The next day, she practically begged Ram to let her go see the other prisoners. Carina saw sorrow on his face when he finally gave in. This time he dropped her off then left immediately, not even pausing to glance back through the window.

It was easy to spot Shaian, sitting at one of the tables. She had a hardened look on her face, as if she was trying to be strong in a universe without hope.

Yeunay was there this time, and Niki still sat close to Shaian. Triska and Kimura were reading off of tablets as Carina approached. There were a few other women around, but Shaian dismissed them with a word. She also gave a look to Triska, but whatever she was trying to communicate, Triska seemed to ignore.

"I have a way off the ship," Carina announced quietly, once the other women were out of earshot.

"Really?" Shaian asked, her face lighting up with a flicker of hope.

Carina leaned forward. "There's a transport — the *Rhincodon* — in the maintenance bay. I saw it on one of my work projects with Ram while it was being repaired. It's a lot more relaxed on security. There's usually not many soldiers guarding that bay."

Shaian looked contemplative. "Is it flyable?"

Carina winced, and shrugged. "That I don't fully know, but they must have almost finished with repairs because I overheard someone talking about moving it to the main bay early next week."

Shaian considered this for some time. The other women looked at her, not wanting to break the silence. Only Triska seemed to not care. She was looking over at the window, and scowling as if she was disappointed Ram wasn't there.

"It's a risk we have to take," Shaian said grimly. "We don't have much time, and we haven't found any other options."

Niki frowned and leaned forward. "What's the rush?"

"We've already started accelerating back toward Varus," Shaian explained. "A transport ship isn't meant for long distance space travel, so we need to leave as soon as possible, so the return trip to Seutura doesn't take too long."

"We wait too long, and we might not make it back at all," Yeunay added, and Shaian nodded.

"We'll do it tomorrow. The sooner the better." Shaian said. "A transport could hold about a hundred or so if we cram into it. It's only a fraction of the prisoners, but it's the best we can do. We'll make our move during dinner. It's the most chaotic time."

"I should be able to slip away then," Carina said, "but how are you guys going to get out of here?"

Shaian grinned. "The door is easy. The zero-g is doable as well, but slow. Don't worry about us. Can you meet us by the maintenance bay?"

Carina nodded. But she had a strange pit in her stomach. Of course she wanted to be free, but as strange as it sounded, she didn't like the feeling that she was betraying Ram by doing this.

Shaian glanced at Kimura. "Have you decided?"

Kimura smiled softly. "Yes. I'm staying."

Yeunay sighed, and Shaian frowned.

"What?" Carina asked, incredulous. The girl must be out of her mind. "Why would you want to stay here, especially knowing that this ship is headed to Varus?"

"Do you know what I experienced back home? Corruption," Kimura said, looking directly at Carina. "My job made me a part of that. I don't want to go back to it. I'm not saying Varus won't have any, but at least there I won't be part of the system. Perhaps I'll be assigned to help a kind family, or even find a job there. I'd rather have that than go back to where I was. I can see myself flourishing if I find a way to be helpful among these people."

Carina regarded her doubtfully. *Unbelievable.* She couldn't imagine being content, let alone happy here, among a strange people. Yes, she had some pleasant times with Ram — the laughter, the ease they'd come to. But could she truly be happy?

The thought struck her oddly. She must be delusional even thinking about it. Caring for the man who had kidnapped her? Ram had treated her nicely for the most part, and war made even good people do wicked things. But she was a prisoner, and he was her captor. Of course she couldn't be happy here.

"You okay?" Yeunay asked, looking across the table at her.

It took Carina a moment to respond. "I'm fine. Just thinking about getting back to Seutura," she lied.

Kimura stood up at that. "Good luck," she said, then headed back to the open cell area.

"That's my cue as well," Triska said, pushing up from her seat.

"You too?" Carina asked.

"I'm with her," Triska said, unapologetically. "Do you know how many fat administrators I've seen skim food off the top when there are people starving two towns over? Besides, if there are only a hundred seats on the transport, I'm not going to take one from someone else." She gave

Carina one last smile. "And who knows, I just might find myself a handsome hunk among the soldiers."

Carina watched the two go, then shook her head. "I guess I just don't understand. Even with our problems, Seutura is home."

It was just Shaian, Niki, Yeunay, and herself now. Strangely she had felt the most camaraderie with Kimura and Triska, and now they were gone.

"We all have to make the best decisions we can, for ourselves," Shaian said, looking at her. "I've been trying to convince those two to come all week. Triska does have a point about spots, but I think the danger is more the number we can get across the zero-g tunnel than seats on the transport."

"Any word of Bryn?" she asked.

Yeunay shook her head. "Nothing. I'm still keeping an eye out for her, but hopefully this just means she wasn't taken in the first place."

"And I won't be taking someone else's seat?" Carina asked Shaian.

"Getting a hundred of us there is unlikely. But even if we can't get everyone, we'll take those who we can. It's our duty to report back to Seutura. We'll plan on meeting at seventeen thirty ship time at the maintenance bay. Try to get there early, though. Once this goes into motion, we can't stop. We've got one shot at this. And as harsh as it sounds, we can't stop for stragglers and risk none of us getting away."

"I understand." And Carina did. She would be there. She was going to go home.

Chapter 23

Ram cursed as the training dummy he'd been pummeling bent at an awkward angle and didn't pop back up. He'd felt ill-tempered all day. He *should* be happy. The *Architeuthis* was headed home. They'd successfully carried out at least a measure of justice for those, like his sister, who had died. He even had Carina coming home with him. What in the ten suns did he have to be irritable about?

A quick glance at the training dummy showed one of the bolts at the bottom had come loose. He stalked across the training room, avoiding the groups currently training and others working there, as he headed for the maintenance closet.

Ram knew *why* he was in a bad mood — and it made him even angrier. Mikael's threats. Thekla's advice. Carina's distress. Her blasted tears.

Thekla and Halvar had been right. He'd lost some perspective. He shouldn't let anyone — let alone an enemy captive — affect him so much.

He keyed open the maintenance closet hatch and yanked out the repair pouch stored inside. He let out a curse as several rolls of sealant tape got knocked loose, which he had to chase and grab.

He shouldn't give a damn if she was upset. Of *course* she was upset. It's not like he thought she was going to be thrilled to get carted back to Varus. It's why he'd waited so blasted long to tell her in the first place.

Ram tossed the sealant rolls back in and mashed down on the keypad to close the hatch to the closet. Tool pouch in hand, he made his way back over to the broken training dummy.

Maybe he was compromised, he realized. The little captive thought she had him wrapped around his finger. Begging to go visit the other prisoners after lunch today. The only reason he'd agree was he needed some time to clear his head and get himself straightened out. Far easier to do that when he didn't have her deep blue eyes haunting him.

He grabbed a multi-wrench from the pouch and crouched beside the broken training dummy.

He wasn't prepared for this. For every bit of him that had viewed Varus taking prisoners as justice, he now had a part of him doubting whether it had been right. Carina had made the enemy personal. Not just a faceless foe, but a fellow human. She was innocent of this, but then again so had his sister been. Did it make it right then?

No. Obviously not. And that was the problem. But now there was no going back. She was stuck here. Why couldn't the blasted woman make the best of it? But with Mikael making threats, Ram had to do something. He needed to keep her in her place, for both their sakes. Distance himself from her. At least for now. Once things settled, once they reached Varus, she might be able to build a life there and thrive, if Halvar and those who sided with him had their way and were able to ensure the Seuturans integrated with their society.

But for now, one wrong step, and Mikael would have him — and Carina — where he wanted.

That made him even more upset.

He slammed down on the broken bolt with the wrench, knocking it out of the space it had gotten jammed into. He fished into the pouch and pulled out a replacement bolt. As he started securing it, he felt himself center and settle.

Yes, that's what he'd do. It's what he had to do. He'd re-establish and enforce their roles. No more observatory and garden trips. No more special tea. He wouldn't allow anything to get back to Mikael that might hint that he cared for her.

Ram watched as the training dummy sprang back up into position and he grunted with satisfaction, trying to ignore the twinge of sadness in his gut. It wouldn't fix everything, but it would do what was needed. It would keep Carina safe.

Chapter 24

Carina was nervous as the soldier led her through the ship back to Ram's quarters. It was unusual that Ram didn't stay to guard her when she spoke with the other prisoners, and that he didn't come to retrieve her made her even more uneasy.

But she was even more anxious to come face to face with him. Now that their escape plan was solidified and they had a meeting time, she felt an almost panic fall over her. Would Ram be able to tell? He was usually so observant. He would know if she was acting off. But she knew the more she tried to *act* normal, the more obvious it would be that she was hiding something.

Perhaps he would just think she was still upset about him lying. She just had to not act too relieved or happy, and he might just chalk up any odd behavior he noticed to that. But it was a risk.

And what if he didn't give her an opportunity to slip away the next night? Dread rose up in her. If she missed the rendezvous, she'd be stuck here for good.

Would that be so bad?

She frowned at the thought. Thoughts like that had been popping into her head ever since she had admitted to herself that she enjoyed her time with Ram. But enjoying time with him wasn't the same as wanting to stay. She might even miss him, but he was taking her away from home. Keeping her from Tennel. She was a captive here, living at the whims of a barbarian people. No matter how nice Ram was at times, she couldn't forget what he was capable of. And the anger he must feel at losing his sister... no, she wasn't safe here.

But you are attracted to him, her thoughts seemed to whisper tauntingly. *You enjoy spending time with him.*

Carina gritted her teeth. That meant *nothing*. Attraction couldn't be the basis of anything meaningful. And there were plenty of people she enjoyed spending time with. But she was his captive. There was no relationship — never would be. At best, she might survive here being useful and flying under the radar. At worst...perhaps Ram *would* take advantage of her one day. And then discard her when she was no longer of any interest to him.

She knew that was a lie, but she held to it anyway. It helped her push on, towards escape. Towards home.

With these anxious thoughts buzzing in her mind, the soldier finally brought her to Ram's door. She was awash with nervous tension.

The soldier pressed a key on the keypad, and a moment later the hatch slid open, revealing a stoic Ram. He nodded his thanks to the soldier as Carina stepped inside.

The door slid shut behind her, and the near-panic returned. How much it reminded her of her first night on board, when they had come here after dinner.

She fought the panic down. She had to act normal. If she wanted any shot at freedom, for herself or the others, she had to hold it together.

When Ram turned to face her, she nearly lost her resolve. There was something in his expression she couldn't place. It was hard, icy and cold, but mixed in with it was something she couldn't decipher. She wanted to call it sadness, but she couldn't figure what he would be sad about that he hadn't been before. She wanted to run over and hug him, to help him and to be held by him at the same time. But she couldn't. It would be better to distance herself from him. To keep herself from giving something away.

There was a long moment of silence, and she struggled to find something normal to say. "Thank you for letting me visit them," she said softly.

If it were possible, the sadness Ram's face grew, but then it was replaced by a hard resolve. She had the brief, panicked worry that perhaps he already knew their plans. Her heart seized.

"It won't happen again for quite a while," he said.

Carina frowned. "Why? I—"

"I don't want you getting used to such freedoms."

Carina flinched back, wondering what he meant. He was acting so different — so distant. She wondered what had happened.

"But—"

"If I want your opinion, I'll inform you."

"Are you okay? Did something happen?" she asked, even more unsure as to his odd behavior.

He came toward her, and was in her face faster than she could react. He gripped the back of her neck, and there was a ferocity in his eyes that made her freeze.

"You are my captive. You don't get to question me. Your opinion, your concerns, are irrelevant. Why have you still not learned that?" Ram pushed away from her roughly, and gestured toward her room. "Go. I'll let you know when you're needed."

Carina stood dumbfounded. Something had changed. She stared at Ram, keeping her face as still as possible. She would *not* cry. Not now. She forced herself to turn and walk calmly to her room. One glance back showed her a glimpse again of the sadness etched on his face. But it hardened as he saw her looking at him.

When the hatch slid shut and she heard the lock engage, she couldn't hold back anymore. Tears welled up in her eyes and came pouring out. How little she'd cried all her years growing up on Seuturan, save for when her mother had died. And yet, in a manner of weeks, she'd cried more than she ever had before in her life. It made her feel weak — and angry.

She didn't know how long she cried. It took a while before she could even process the situation.

Was this the real him? She had thought she was getting to know him, getting through his toughened exterior. But he was Varusian. A soldier. Loyal to his planet. Even if he disagreed with an order, he would follow them. She wondered how sad he would be if they ordered him to kill her. She wanted to believe he would refuse, but she was uncertain. Was that someone she wanted to go back to Varus with?

His words cut deep, even if she was sure she caught a hint of reluctance in his face. It made her even more angry — at herself. She knew better than to get attached, and still she had. She'd let herself be lured in by his charm, annoyingly attracted despite his sometimes gruff nature. For the briefest of moments she had hoped there was a chance for something, but it was clear now that there wasn't. How foolish had she been.

Had he even felt anything similar to what she had felt towards him? She had almost thought she understood him when he had talked about his sister. The pain he must have felt.

But how well could she really understand a Varusian? She was Seuturan. His captive.

She swiped at her tears, taking a deep breath. It didn't matter. She wouldn't have to deal with the brute much longer anyway. Her resolve at escaping hardened, any doubts wiped away.

A little over twenty-four hours, and she'd be on her way back home and freedom.

Chapter 25

The next day, Carina was filled with nervous tension. The butterflies started as soon as she woke up. Ram's cool aloofness exacerbated it even more. He mostly ignored her and hardly said a word to her, other than to snap abrupt instructions.

There was no lid on her cup of tea at breakfast, and he had dumped her half-finished mug in the cleanser when she didn't finish before he was done with his food. During training, when she normally got to sit, watch, and chat with a few of the other assigned captives, he had her clean a portion of the locker room. Rather than protest — or hit him over the head with the cleansing mop, which was what her first impulse had been — she quietly went about the work, a calm determination settling over her.

After lunch, Ram silently led her to their afternoon assignment — organizing one of the food storage units. She quietly sorted packets of dried fruits that had gotten jumbled, while Ram moved some of the bulkier food storage crates around. She caught herself peeking over at him every once in a while as they worked, fighting the inclination to banter with him as usual. Each time she realized what she was doing, she forced herself to work harder. To ignore him while she sorted.

She knew it was for the best to stay distant — only a few hours to go — but she still felt disappointed by the frigid silence between them. Part of her wanted to apologize again for his sister, even though she had no direct role in what had happened. Part of her wanted to go up and slap him, to knock some sense into him. Anything, just to get some reaction from him, to make her leaving feel less of a betrayal.

Her resolve for silence weakened at that. She was leaving. Even if he was being an ass, she had to say *something*. She was still trying to figure out what to say, and working up the courage to do so, when Ram let out a curse as the awkward, bulky bags he was trying to lift up on a storage shelf started to slip.

Carina was up and across the room before she had time to think, reaching up to try to help steady the top of the five flour bags he was trying to lift.

"Get back," he growled at her.

She scowled. "Don't be an idiot. I'm just trying to help."

"I don't need your blasted help."

"Well, if you weren't trying to grab so many at a time—"

"I said get back!"

As Ram tried to step back away from her, the top bag slipped toward her. It slammed into her, knocking her to the floor. A blinding pain shot through her ankle as the bag came to rest awkwardly on her leg. They were heavy. How had he managed to lift five at once?

"Damn the Founders," Ram cursed, tossing the remaining bags in his arms to the floor behind him. He yanked the bag off of her leg and crouched down.

Carina winced as she tried to move her foot.

"Are you alright?"

"Does it look like I'm alright?" she snapped, fighting back tears. The pain was bad, but the dread building up inside her was even worse. She had to be able to get up and move. If she couldn't make it to the meeting point for the escape…

With the panic of that thought echoing through her mind, she started to push herself up.

"Wait, I need to see if it's—"

"I'm fine!" Carina said.

Ram held her shoulders firmly, and anger lit his face. "You would have been fine if you'd just listened. I told you to stay back."

"Well, I'm sorry for trying to help!" she shot back.

Ram snarled something under his breath, then moved closer. She tried to scramble back, but pain shot up her leg. Before she could protest, Ram scooped her up into his arms and rose. He made his way toward the storage room exit.

Panic filled her, and she pushed against his chest. "Wait — no, wait, I'm fine—"

"No, you're not," Ram growled. "I'm taking you to the medbay."

Fear gripped her. Would she be able to escape from there? She had hoped to slip away at dinner. She wasn't sure there would be a good opportunity to get away from inside the medbay. Why, why, had she decided to try to help the stupid brute in the first place?

"No, please Ram," she said, hating herself for the pathetic pleading she couldn't keep from her voice. She couldn't get stuck here. She couldn't.

"Stars, woman, you'd think I was bringing you to your death," Ram said, surliness evident in his voice.

She wanted to shout at him that he might as well be, but she bit her tongue. "Why do you even care?"

"Need to make sure it's not a bad injury or broken," he said, glowering as he stared straight ahead. He continued at a quick pace down the corridor, refusing to look down at her. "Can't have a defective captive."

Carina scoffed. "I'm sure you could just trade me in for a better one."

"Maybe I'll get one who can listen to my blasted orders."

"Docile, sweet, and does as they're told?"

He snarled, but didn't say anything more.

She grimaced. Somehow his silence hurt more than any remark. She should be glad he didn't want her. Ignorant barbarian.

She stayed stiff in his arms, forcing herself not to relax, as he walked briskly through the ship. And, she told herself as they entered a lift, the comfort of his arms, being pressed against his hard, muscled chest did *not* feel good. Ram stared at the lift door as the numbers on the keypad flashed by, his face tense. In this close proximity, she caught a whiff of him — citrus and sweat and cloves — that made her just want to press herself closer against him. She closed her eyes, trying to battle away the waring emotions she felt inside her. She couldn't lose her resolve now.

They finally reached the medbay, and Ram deposited her onto one of the beds, far more gently than his attitude belayed. He snapped at a woman — another captive, by the look of her clothing — who was filling up a supply station nearby.

The woman, dark brown hair framing her face and haunted green eyes, flinched back from Ram, nearly cringing with fear.

Carina put a hand on Ram's arm. "Stop it! You're scaring people!" He shook off her touch.

Scowling, he said to the woman, "Get over here and check out her leg!"

A medic — the one with a limp that helped her her first day here — came up behind the fearful woman and set a hand gently on her shoulder. She tensed even more for a brief moment, then relaxed. But she didn't take her wide eyes off Ram.

"Ram, don't speak to my assistant that way," the medic said in a mild tone, but there was an edge to it, and a dangerous glint in his eyes.

"Then get over here and check out her leg, Stefan."

Stefan stood a moment, looking at Ram. Then he whispered something in the woman's ear, and she nodded briefly. With one more glance at Ram, she turned and walked to another part of the medbay.

"What happened?" Stefan asked, moving close. He gave Carina's foot an assessing look.

"A bag of flour fell on me," Carina said.

"Because you can't blasted follow directions," Ram growled.

"But," Carina said, shooting a glare at Ram, "it's mostly just my ankle that hurts. I think it's fine."

"Well, let's take a look," Stefan said. He eased her shoe off and reached for a small scanner device that was docked beside the med bed. He held it over her ankle and foot, then turned her foot slightly. She hissed in pain, and Stefan gave her an apologetic look.

"You going to hurt her more or are you going to fix the damn thing?" Ram said, his fists clenching at the edges of the med bed. Stefan gave him a contemplative look, but didn't respond. He continued to calmly work on the sensor display. He seemed unphased by Ram's behavior. Perhaps he was used to dealing with unruly people in the medbay.

"Eira," Stefan called out across the room. "Could you please bring me a medwrap and a tube of numbing cream?" He looked at Carina and Ram. "Doesn't appear broken, but it's a bad sprain."

Carina felt relief course through her. Not broken. She still had a chance.

The Seuturan woman, Eira, arrived with a folded piece of thick, white cloth and a small silver tube. She looked unsure, watching Ram from the corner of her eye. Carina wondered if she was being treated poorly. Her eyes were wary and full of fear. She handed the tube to Stefan and he began to work. Eira seemed more comfortable closer to Stefan. It didn't seem like the medic was mistreating her at least. But she always moved in a way that kept Ram in her peripheral vision. Stefan squeezed something out of the tube and began applying the cool cream around Carina's ankle.

Eira unraveled the wrap, her hands shaking, and she nearly dropped it in the process.

Ram grumbled under his breath. "Are you competent, girl? Give me that if you can't manage." Ram reached for the wrap, and Eira jerked back, slamming against the med-bed beside them, terror evident on her face. The impact seemed to startle her less than Ram reaching for her had, but she still slid to the ground, shaking.

Carina looked at Ram, aghast. He'd been in a bad mood before, but she'd never seen him acting so rudely to anyone. What had gotten into him?

Stefan stepped between Ram and Eira, forcing Ram's attention to him. Ram dwarfed the medic, but Stefan didn't seem to care. His jaw clenched, and for the first time Carina saw anger in his eyes as he looked at Ram.

"You may not ever speak to her like that again," Stefan said, his voice utterly calm, but with such a dangerous edge that even Ram looked taken aback.

"Stefan—" Ram started to say, as it seemed he finally realized he was behaving badly.

"Get out of the medbay," Stefan said, emphasizing every word, "or I'll call security and have you taken to the brig"

Ram's jaw clenched, but he didn't say a word. He turned around with just a quick glance at Carina and stalked out of the medbay. She heard his steps fade down the corridor.

Stefan helped Eira up, whispering something to her that Carina could not make out. She seemed comforted by his presence and words, and her shaking lessened until it became manageable.

"I'm so sorry," Carina said to Eira. "I don't know what's gotten into him."

"It's okay," Eira said, smiling at Carina as she reached down to pick up the wrap.

"No, it's not," Stefan said. He was calm, but Carina could hear the underlying anger simmering beneath the surface. It surprised her. Was he angry that Ram had been rude to a captive?

Eira began wrapping Carina's ankle with sure, smooth movements. She seemed much calmer now that Ram was gone, and her hands no longer shook. Eira gave Stefan a look and smile. "It's not his fault I'm so jumpy."

"No, but it's his fault for running his mouth and acting like an ass," Stefan said, capping the tube of numbing cream, and making his way back across the medbay.

"Are you sure you're okay?" Carina asked Eira. "He can be grumpy sometimes, but I've never seen him so aggressive toward someone outside of training."

"It's really okay," Eira said, adjusting the wrap. "It was clear he was just worried about you."

Carina let out a snort. "Not likely. Maybe worried I'll be defective." She looked at the woman, unsure exactly what to say. "But he wouldn't hurt you."

"I know," Eira said, attaching the end of the wrap and pressing the seal closed. "I'm sorry I'm so jumpy. I was... attacked, shortly after coming on board." Carina took in a sharp breath, horrified, then shot a glance at Stefan. Eira followed her gaze, shaking her head. "No, Stefan saved me. He's been very kind. And protective," she added, smiling softly.

"I'm so sorry," Carina said, shaking her head.

"It's okay. I'm getting better. Just...volatile situations sometimes make me...uneasy."

Carina smiled. "He's kinder than he looks. Usually, at least."

Eira laughed. Stefan seemed to have calmed down as well. "You may be right, but that doesn't excuse him at all," he said. "He can be a bit stubborn sometimes. He gets an idea in his head, and doesn't know when to let it go."

Carina felt uneasy at that. Was he saying that Ram needed to let *her* go? Let go of his feelings for her? Or was he saying something else?

"You'll need to rest up for the rest of the day," Stefan continued. "I'll call someone down to escort you back up to your quarters."

Carina felt a stab of panic, and she started to push herself off the bed. "No, I think I'm good!" she said brightly. If she got locked in her quarters, there would be no chance she'd be able to slip away tonight.

Stefan frowned, but Eira placed a hand on his arm. "I could escort her back." He looked at her, softening immediately.

"You can go with her, but you need someone with you as well," Stefan said. He reached for a comm device, and gave Eira a look. "Is Jansci okay?"

Eira nodded, a small smile on her lips. The haunting that appeared in her eyes was gone. For the moment at least.

While Stefan commed for an escort, Eira helped Carina get her shoe back on and get on her feet. Carina gingerly tried to put weight on her foot and winced.

"It will take a little while for the numbing cream to start working," Eira told her. "Are you sure you don't want to rest here for a while?"

"I'm okay," Carina insisted. "I'd really rather rest in my room." If she got back soon enough, she could convince Ram to take her to dinner. It would be more difficult to slip away with her injury, but she would make it work. She had to.

A few minutes later, a soldier with graying hair and a closely clipped beard arrived. He introduced himself as Corporal Jansci. He seemed to know Eira, and she was nowhere near as jumpy with him as she had been with Ram. Carina leaned slightly on Eira for support while they followed the soldier back toward the quarters. Carina tried to remain hopeful. She just had to convince Ram she felt fine enough to walk to dinner.

By the time they reached Ram's quarters, the pain had dulled significantly, and she no longer needed to lean on Eira for support.

"Thank you," she said to Eira, who smiled back at her.

But when Jansci keyed open Ram's door, Ram was nowhere to be seen.

"Corporal Ram informed me to ensure you got to your room and said you needed to rest up," the soldier said. Carina felt the edges of panic creep up into her.

"But, he'll come get me for dinner?" Carina asked.

The soldier shrugged, looking mildly apologetic. She was going to be locked in her room. If Ram didn't come get her for dinner — which was looking likely if he'd sent orders to rest up with the soldier who had escorted her — she would miss the escape rendezvous.

"But—" she started to say, willing herself to stay calm. If she panicked now, and started acting too suspiciously, she could ruin the escape for everyone.

"Just have my orders, Miss," the soldier said, his face stern.

"Of course," Carina said softly, stomach plummeting. She forced back tears.

"Let me help her get settled in at least." Eira said. Jansci nodded, shooting a kind smile back at her.

"That's fine. I'll wait here." He stood by the entrance to Ram's quarters at attention.

Eira followed Carina to her room.

"It will be alright," Eira said softly as they entered. "Stefan had told me about Ram. He seems to be a good, honorable soldier. It's an adjustment for everyone, hmm?"

Carina wondered if Eira was trying to assure herself or Carina more. The woman was obviously traumatized by her assault. She must have been the woman Carina had heard about that was attacked the first night she was here. She wanted to assure Eira as well. She gave a smile she didn't feel, but the words felt genuine as they came out. "He is. He really is."

Eira cocked her head slightly. "You care for him?"

Carina scoffed. "Hardly. I mean, he's been...nice, all things considered. But I wouldn't even be here if it weren't for him."

Eira nodded as she helped Carina over to the bed. She could already tell how kind and caring Eira was even after just spending a few minutes with her. If Carina couldn't escape, then at least Eira should be able to.

"Have you heard about what some of the captives are going to try tonight?" Carina asked carefully.

Eira drew a breath and nodded. "Seventeen thirty at the maintenance bay," she said. "I hope that everyone who wants to go can make it."

"I hope most of us will," Carina said as she sat down on her bed. "There's little hope for me."

"Don't despair," Eira added softly. "There's always hope."

With that Eira got up to leave. Carina watched as she left and the door slid shut. She heard the outer door close as well.

Hope. Not likely.

She sank back into the bed and put her face in her hands. Unless by some miracle Ram came back and got her for dinner, she had no hope. It wasn't like she was going to find any other means of transportation to escape back to Seutura.

Carina's head jerked up, and her gaze shot to the shut hatch of her room.

A half-thought crossed her mind, bringing her heartbeat up a tick. She realized there was a sound she hadn't heard as Eira left. She tried to keep herself calm as she keyed open her hatch. She stepped over to the main quarter's hatch that led to the corridor outside. Ram always kept it locked. But what if...

She took a deep breath, then reached out and pressed down on the keypad.

The door slid open with a satisfying hiss, and Carina let out an unsteady breath. She had no idea how Eira had managed it, but she must have done something. Had she distracted the soldier? Convinced him to keep the door unlocked? She had no idea, but she thanked the stars as she stepped out into the corridor. There was still hope.

Chapter 26

As Ram walked back to his quarters, carrying a dinner tray with water and extra dessert balanced on top, he was feeling the uncomfortable twinges of regret.

Guilt had been a familiar companion since the death of his sister eight months ago, but this felt different. That had fed a passion for revenge — one he had purposefully stroked up until the attack on Seutura. It had burned bright even once he saw the face of his enemy. But, even then, dousing had begun. As its flame died, what he was left with was emptiness. And then something had begun to fill that. *Someone.* When he realized she might get taken away...

Of course it was necessary to put some distance between himself and the girl, but he realized he'd approached it the wrong way. He had started far too heavy handed with the whole thing. The distance could be temporary, after all. Perhaps back on Varus things could be better. He had been too hard on her today.

Of course, if she wasn't so stubborn, she wouldn't have put herself in a position to get hurt.

He found himself several paces behind two captives, a man and a woman, both dressed in honey-yellow. The sight of two captives together — unusual, though not completely odd — gave him pause, and disrupted the path of his thoughts. He overheard one of them quietly say something about the "...*Rhincodon* at seventeen thirty."

His brow furrowed slightly. He thought the *Rhincodon* was still in maintenance. But perhaps they were assigned to someone who was part of an evening team that was trying to wrap up repairs.

But that only occupied his thoughts for a moment. By the time he neared his quarters, he had circled back to the problem at hand. If he was careful, it could all still work out. There had to be *some* distance, though, for her own good. He would keep her safe from Mikael. They just had to settle into their roles for now and eventually everything would be fine.

He squared his shoulders and keyed open his hatch. Stefan had commed him fifteen minutes ago to let him know that he'd just sent her back with Eira and Corporal Jansci, with instructions to rest.

The living space of his quarters was empty, but he figured she would be in her room. Ram knocked on her hatch. "I've got dinner," Ram called out. There was no response. "And some extra dessert. Chocolate cheesecake." *That* ought to get to her. She loved the stuff.

When silence greeted him, he scowled. She was probably sulking. He debated whether to just key the door open anyway, and make her take the blasted food. But he hesitated. Maybe she was just resting. She had gotten hurt fairly badly today.

He stood there a moment, debating what to do. He nearly just set the tray down in front of the door so she could get it later if she awoke hungry. But something in him pushed him to check on her — to make sure she was okay. An image of her curled up crying on her bed struck his mind, and it cut into him like a Hapei phase blade. He reached out and keyed open the door.

He frowned as he took in the dark room. Light from the living area lit up a small portion of the space, revealing an empty room. The bed showed no signs of being disturbed. He turned the lights on, only to confirm his fears.

"Buttercup?" he called out, glancing around. The chair was empty too. He took two strides to get to the bathroom. Nothing. She wasn't here.

He was baffled. Even as injured as she was, it shouldn't have taken Jansci much more than five minutes to escort her from medbay to here. Had he misunderstood Stefan's comm?

And then his heart stopped.

A thought took hold in his mind, blooming into suspicion and dread. He was already moving toward the door to his quarters before it could fully root in his mind, apprehension haunting his every step. If he was right, he just had to hope he wasn't too late.

Chapter 27

She tried not to wince as she took another step. The numbing cream wasn't a full anesthetic and she wasn't supposed to be walking on her ankle. The terror of potential discovery didn't help either.

At every turn, every lift ride, every walkway, Carina anticipated that someone would realize what she was doing and grab her. That a prisoner would be discovered missing and someone would sound an alert.

But no one so much as glanced at her with suspicion. In the past six weeks, the captives who had been claimed had seemed to blend well with the crew, and while it wasn't common to see one by themselves unescorted, no one seemed to find it odd that she walked freely in the ship's corridors.

It helped, she knew, that it was dinner time. Shaian had been wise to choose this as the time to escape. Most crew members were making their way to the dining hall, still in good spirits that they were on their way home to Varus. Besides, what harm could they imagine that a lone Seuturan woman would cause?

Carina kept her eyes down, tried to disguise her wounded foot, and stayed determined to just keep moving.

By the time she neared the maintenance bay, her foot was throbbing, and the pain radiated part way up her calf. She tried to keep her breathing even as she pushed through the pain.

At this point, the number of crew members had thinned significantly, most having already made their way to dinner, leaving only the few essential personnel who were still on duty behind.

She had one more long corridor to go, and then she would arrive. The rendezvous point was a small ready room just across and to the side of the hangar. It was far enough from any guards that might be posted, and in an area that wouldn't be completely unusual for a claimed captive to be in. It would be safe until enough captives arrived to make their gathering noticeable. Hopefully by then it would only be a few minutes before they were ready to leave the ship.

Carina kept her head down as she walked the last stretch of corridor to the ready room. Just a few meters down, she nearly collided with a crew member coming from the opposite direction. She flinched back, surprised he had chosen to walk so close to her when the hallway was otherwise empty.

"Hello there, love," the man said, stopping short. Carina took a sharp breath as her eyes lifted and she spotted the white uniform and sharp-featured face she recognized. Mikael, the command officer who had given Ram a hard time. She tried to keep the panic at bay. It didn't help that her foot was throbbing.

He gave her a look that made her want to wash herself for a week. "Ah, I had thought it was you. Ram's girl," he said. She wanted to snap that she wasn't anyone's, but she bit her tongue. She needed to get around him without incident.

Thankfully she'd had time on the journey to come up with a convincing story. She gestured beyond him. "Ram forgot his...helmet. He sent me to retrieve it," she said, trying to keep her voice steady, despite her pounding heart. And desperately trying not to show any uncertainty. All he had to do was comm in a message, and she was done for. Along with everyone else.

Her heart beat wildly in her chest. She fought to keep her breathing even — which would have been a much easier task if it weren't for the stabbing pain in her ankle.

Mikael tsked, stepping closer to her. "He sent you off all by yourself?" Carina resisted the urge to take a step backwards.

"I need to get going, otherwise I'm going to get in trouble," she said, not looking him in the eye. "If you'll excuse me—" She moved to step around him.

His arm shot out, grabbing onto hers. "No need to hurry, love. I'm sure Ram wouldn't mind if you took a little extra time."

"I really think he would." Carina tugged, trying to free her arm, the panic rising. His grip was like iron, unrelenting. Would screaming for help do anything? She was just as likely to draw the wrong attention — and possibly reveal the captives gathering — as she was to be helped.

Mikael's grip tightened, and he moved closer, an unmistakably dangerous look on his face.

"If you touch me, Ram will kill you," Carina said, tensing. The fear was nearly paralyzing at this point. She needed to get away, and get away now.

Mikael laughed. "He won't do anything to me. He's just a lowly soldier. I just have to say the word, and he'll be thrown into the brig, even kicked out of the army." He pulled her in closer, up against his body, leering. "Then perhaps I'll keep you for myself. You look like you'd be some fun." He reached for her face with his free hand.

Carina brought her knee up just like Ram had shown her. She wasn't at an ideal angle, but it caught him by surprise and made contact. He grunted, but his grip on her arm didn't loosen. Then she brought her free arm up in a jab, going for his throat.

Her aim was off though, and she cursed herself for not practicing more with Ram. After that first lesson they had only done one more. He had seemed less enthused about it, and she had thought it was a waste of time and hadn't insisted on continuing. Now she was regretting it.

Her arm moved past Mikael's neck, not even glancing against it. Once she realized she had missed she tried to use her momentum, pulling to the side with her whole weight, trying desperately to escape his grasp.

His grip didn't weaken and he recovered quickly from her poor attacks, yanking her back against him. "Oh, you're going to pay for that," he said in her ear.

Before the fear of what his words meant could sink in, the loud explosive crackle of blaster fire echoed through the corridor, and Mikael jerked. Then his grip was gone, and she spun away, shaking.

A man, dressed in captives clothing stood at the far end of the hall, holding a blaster. Carina nearly cried with relief when she saw Shaian beside him. She looked down. Mikael lay on the ground, groaning. Blood spread out from a wound on his back, seeping across his white uniform. She stood frozen for a moment, hands shaking.

She felt numb. A man was bleeding out in front of her. But she had to move. Freedom was so close. Just down the corridor. She looked over at Shaian and the man with the gun and started limping down the hall toward them. It was just the two of them on the opposite end of the corridor, but she could see a few other captives in the hangar, heading towards the *Rhincodon*.

Before she had taken three steps, a black blur hurtled through the large hatchway near the captives at the far end of the corridor. The soldier lashed out in a smooth arc with his arm, catching the hand of the man with the weapon and sent the blaster skittering down the hallway. The captive stumbled back, and for a moment there was no other movement. After a brief moment of hesitation, Shaian and the other captives turned and ran into the bay. But the soldier didn't pursue them.

Carina's heart stopped as he turned to face her, but she already knew who it was.

Ram.

No. *No*. She was so close to freedom.

"Buttercup…" Ram said, slowly approaching her.

"Why do you have to ruin everything?" she asked, tears coming to her eyes.

He stopped two meters from her, his eyes tracing over her as if he was making sure she was in one piece. His gaze flicked behind her, to Mikael bleeding on the floor. But he didn't move.

"Are you okay?" he asked, his gaze darting back to her.

"No!"

Ram stiffened. "Did he hurt you?"

"What? I…no…"

The tension in his shoulders eased a fraction, and he looked over his shoulder at the captives in the maintenance bay crowding into the *Rhincodon*. He hesitated for just a moment. When he turned back toward her, she saw sorrow flicker across his face before his jaw set. He stepped forward and reached for her.

She flinched back, but he reacted faster, his hands shooting out to grip her arm.

"You need to go."

"What?" Her mind reeled.

"You don't have much time." He tugged her lightly, trying to draw her closer to the maintenance bay entrance. Was this a trick?

"Why? What are you doing?" He was a Varusian soldier. Even if he wanted to let her go, he couldn't. This *must* be a trick. But she let him lead her — didn't have the energy to resist. Ram's hand was steady on her as her heart raced. She took one step, and then another.

"Because revenge isn't all it's cracked up to be," he said, the sorrow coming out in his voice. "Because even though you've been an ass once it doesn't mean you always have to be an ass." Ram glanced back at her, giving her a small, sad smile. "And because even the most beautiful flower will die without its sun."

The corridor felt far too short. Before she knew it she stood at the entrance to the bay. Doubt filled her mind. Not doubt about Ram's motives now, but about her decision. Ram had shifted his arm around her to support her and ease the pain of her ankle. His arm was firm but gentle, and his chest was reassuring as she leaned against it. His scent, citrus and clove woven together with what she imagined starlight would smell like.

"You'll get in trouble," she said, as they stopped at the end of the corridor. She turned to look at him. His arm shifted around her waist, but he didn't quite let go.

"You let me worry about that," he said looking down at her. For a moment Carina was lost in his eyes. "You have a transport to catch."

It felt like a blow to her gut.

"But —"

"You don't have much time. It'll take five minutes to get the transport warmed up and ready to fly. You don't want to miss it."

She looked between him and the *Rhincodon*. He was right. She wouldn't have a real life here. Even with him, she couldn't expect to be treated as a person at Varus. She had to get going, but when she looked back at him, she hesitated again.

"Go," he said. "Go back to the sunlight."

Freedom. She was trapped here. Trapped with him, but trapped. She needed to go.

Her heart stuttered, and she rose up on her toes to kiss him softly on the cheek. He just stared down at her with a small, sad smile on his face. It took an effort to pull away. What held her wasn't his grip, but some portion of her heart. He had given her exactly what she'd been longing for. But she didn't know why escaping now filled her with such sorrow.

She stepped back, unable to turn around. It took two more steps before she could pry her eyes off of him and turn. She hurried through the maintenance bay. The ramp to the transport was still down. She turned as she reached it, back towards Ram. He was too far away for her to make out his face, but she saw the tension in his stance, before he turned and disappeared from her view.

She turned back to the *Rhincodon* and rushed up the ramp.

Freedom. She was going home.

Chapter 28

The blare of a priority alarm on his comm came as he sat in the darkness of his quarters. Ram had managed to rig an anonymous message about a downed officer before getting away from the *Rhincodon*. It wouldn't do him any good to be found over Mikael's wounded body or anywhere near the maintenance bay where the prisoners had escaped. Mikael would most likely live. There was a lot of blood, but the wound didn't look like it had struck anything vital. Ram had seen people survive worse.

Apprehension pulled at him from every side, like the vacuum of space. He couldn't seem to slow the frantic staccato of his heart. There was nothing he could do. Hopefully the alarm was just for Mikael, and not for the *Rhincodon* just yet. The transport couldn't avoid detection for more than a few minutes more. But at this point he had done all he could by letting them go. He couldn't help them — couldn't help *her* — more than he already had.

He just sat in the darkness, counting every minute as thoughts of Carina flooded his mind. He would never see her smile again, smell the fresh, floral scent of her hair, enjoy the sounds of her laughter, or her conversation.

Gone. She was gone. And he had let her go.

The alarm had been blaring for almost a minute before he finally looked at it. He was relieved at what it read.

"Escaped prisoners. Check status of captives."

Nothing about the *Rhincodon* yet.

He keyed back a message on the comm indicating that Carina could not be found. No use in trying to hide it now.

He waited another couple minutes before heading out to the *Architeuthis* command center where the alert ordered him to report. The entire time, he inwardly wrestled with his doubts. Had he made the right decision? The rational part of him knew he had, but it was the decision that removed her from his life, the one who had started to fill the void in his life, and he couldn't quite come to terms with that. Strangely, his betrayal of Varus came a distant second to that revelation.

When he stepped into the observation deck he could feel the tension in the air. The deck wrapped around half of the command center, which gave those on it the ability to both see and hear what was going on below. Rows of chairs allowed for more than a couple hundred people to be there at once.

Despite it being its own deck, the front row was only separated from the command center floor by a few stairs. The larged curved area that connected it to the command center could be closed off by a retractable darkening window, but right now the window wasn't in place. A number of higher ups in the white command uniforms stood near a status table in the center of the room. Data streamed on the surface, and a number of holos hovered above, including one of the *Rhincodon*. Ram forced himself to stay calm and keep his breaths steady and his face impassive.

He stood in the back, behind the last row of chairs and away from the doors. The last thing he wanted was to give something away. The commotion of the officers filling the room only let him hide for about a minute. Before he knew it Thekla had appeared leaning against the wall next to him. "Any news?" Ram asked, casually.

Thekla shot him a look that was far too perceptive. *Damn.* He shouldn't act too calm.

"Group of captives took the *Rhincodon* from the maintenance bay," Thekla said. "One of ours was wounded during the escape. He's in medbay now — looks like he's going to make it."

"Any of the prisoners apprehended or hurt during the escape?" Ram asked. He hoped the hint of nervousness in his voice might help satisfy Thekla.

"A few were traveling together — looks like they were running late to whatever rendezvous they had planned — and were caught." Ram's chest tightened, hoping that those prisoners wouldn't face too harsh a punishment. Thekla gave him a look. "Your girl was involved?"

Ram's jaw clenched, and he chose his words carefully. "Looks like it. I'm at fault. I didn't ensure she was secure before I...got us dinner."

The hesitation cost him.

"Ram..." Thekla said, giving him a hard look. He lowered his voice, but it did nothing to temper the sharpness. "What in the black void of space did you do?"

Ram sighed. He should have known it was hopeless to fool Thekla. He knew him better than he knew himself sometimes.

"I let her go back to the sunshine," he muttered, glancing around the deck.

A moment of silence filled the air, as if Thekla was trying to figure out what impostor had replaced Ram.

"What kind of asinine...?" Thekla growled. "You know what, nevermind." Then he gave Ram a sharp look. "The wounded soldier?"

"Mikael." Thekla's eyes narrowed. "And before you ask, unfortunately no, it wasn't me."

Thekla cursed. "Anyone see you?"

Ram shook his head. "I stuck to the back corridors and my comm unit was back in my quarters, so no one can place me there."

"Starfighters have been mobilized."

"Starfighters?" Ram shot a sharp look at Thekla, then toward the officers through the window. "They aren't planning on attacking it, are they?"

"There's been discussion," Thekla said.

"Those are prisoners of war." Surely they wouldn't attack an unarmed vessel full of captives, even if they had escaped.

"Who escaped, no thanks to you." The *you idiot* was implied in Thekla's voice. "And may have stolen valuable intel with them."

"Is there evidence of that?" Ram asked.

Thekla gave him a look, and Ram ground his teeth.

Admiral Untamo stepped through the doorway from the command center and into the conference room. While the raiding operation only consisted of a single ship, it had been important enough of a mission to send Admiral Untamo along. The admiral didn't look like an imposing man at first glance. He was of average height and stature, and a bald head that gleamed in the light of the monitors. His face held the weathered look of a man who had been into the Abyss. But it was in his eyes that one could see the wisdom and shrewd intelligence that earned him the admiralship.

Conversation came to an abrupt halt, and all eyes turned to him.

"As I'm sure most of you are aware, at approximately seventeen forty hours a number of prisoners escaped on one of our transports," Admiral Untamo said. "Lieutenant Commander Mikael was injured during the escape. He's currently recovering in medbay. Once he regains consciousness, we're hoping to get more information from him. We're also working on compiling a list to ascertain the number of captives who escaped."

Untamo paused, clasping his hands behind his back. "We aren't sure if the prisoners escaped with any valuable intel or military technology, though we have no reason to believe so at this time. Still, the transport itself is much more advanced than Seuturan technology. Our starfighters are six minutes out."

Ram's chest tightened.

"You don't plan to shoot down war prisoners, Admiral?" a voice called out. Ram let out a breath of air. It was Havlar, being the voice of reason like usual.

"Why not, commander?" Captain Kasperi asked, a slight sneer playing on his hatchet-like face. He was a tall man, nearly a head taller than the admiral, and a head full of russet hair pulled back in a short ponytail. He and Mikael were frequent confidants, and Kasperi would be out for blood over Mikael's injuries. Not that he was the type that needed an excuse for violence. "They attacked one of our commanding officers. We can't risk them getting back to Seutura with any valuable information. Who cares about a few Seuturan lives?"

Thekla's arm was across his chest before Ram had even realized he'd stepped forward. "I think you've already done enough damage. Don't lose your temper here," Thekla said quietly.

"I'm not going to let them shoot down the transport," Ram said through clenched teeth. He had let her go on it. He couldn't let her die because of him.

"Not going to do a lot of good if you get yourself thrown into the brig for assaulting a superior officer," Thekla reminded him.

Ram glared at Thekla. He couldn't stand here and wait, but Thekla's fierce look made him hesitate a moment. He heard the argument continuing on the floor before him.

"...plenty of hostages still aboard," Halvar was saying.

"Have you gone that soft?" Kasperi asked. "I expected more from the hero of Kelton."

The word rang out, like throwing a stun grenade in the room. Kelton was loaded with emotion. It was recent enough to be well burnt into people's memories, and just distant enough for there to be doubts about all the decisions made during it.

"That is precisely why he should speak," Untamo said firmly, breaking the tense atmosphere. "We are all well aware of Kelton. My son fought and died there."

Ram took a deep breath. Untamo was of Hapei. While Untamo had stayed loyal to the throne, it was Hapei that had rebelled and fought on the other side at Kelton. His son had fought on the side of his faction. Ram had always thought of Untamo as an honorable man, but revenge for a family member's death could cloud judgment. Ram would know.

"Our decision today must be about what is best for us long term," Halvar said.

Untamo nodded at that. "Petty revenge should never be our goal. We should always have a larger picture in mind." Ram couldn't decipher his inflection. Was he hiding his true intent behind his words? Untamo glanced back toward the command room and called out, "ETA on our starfighters?"

"Three minutes."

Kasperi scoffed. "The larger picture *is* Varus. The Seuturans are a bunch of weaklings. We'd have been better off invading and beating them into submission, rather than this whole theater."

"We'd be no better than them, attacking innocents," Ram called out across the room. From the corner of his eye, he saw Thekla raise his hand to his head.

Kasperi tilted his head, looking at Ram with a predatory grin. "Corporal, I saw your captive is one of those who escaped. With your competence in question, I don't believe you have a voice in this discussion."

Thekla put a hand on his shoulder, and Ram bit back several things he wanted to say to the captain. At this point going back and forth with Kasperi would do more harm than good. It took all his willpower to do it.

"Regardless of Corporal Ram's captive's involvement," Admiral Untamo interrupted, "this decision must be made carefully."

"Starfighters coming in range, fifty kilometers," the warrant officer called from the other room. Untamo turned his attention back to the command table. Kasperi had made his way over to Untamo, and was talking with him.

Ram was envisioning what Kasperi's face would look like after he had him for just five minutes when Thekla's comm beeped. He stepped away from Ram.

Ram kept his eyes locked on the command room, straining to hear the murmured conversation around the table. He ignored a smug look Kasperi shot in his direction. Admiral Untamo looked to still be weighing options even as the display for the distance of the fighters ticked down. Ram held his breath. The fighters were all but on top of the transport. He felt, in that moment, the same helplessness he'd felt when he'd received the comm message about his sister's death. What could he do? He clenched his fists. Assaulting Kasperi might land him in the brig, but it would get his opinion across. He was about to move forward, when Thekla's hand grabbed his shoulder.

"Don't stop me," Ram growled.

"Wait, Ram," Thekla said, pointing.

Ram looked in the midst of the room. Halvar was standing next to Untamo. The two were in discussion. Untamo was shaking his head looking at the display, a look of dismay covering his face. Had Halvar done it? Did he get Untamo to see reason? If Untamo called it off, Ram would etch him into his armor.

"Starfighters, stand down," Untamo called out. Ram let out a breath, relief flooding him. Carina was alive. She would be okay.

But the relief was momentary, replaced by the knowledge that she was truly gone from his life.

Chapter 29

He stared into the golden depths of the glass in front of him, swirling it slowly. He sat in a small, lone illuminated section of the mess hall. The rest was in darkness, save for the dim emergency lights running along the bottom edges of the floor. The room smelled strongly of cleaner and disinfectant from the cleaning crew that had come through earlier.

The table Ram sat at was right up against the wall, a large viewing screen on the bulkhead in front of him displaying the stars outside.

He didn't often indulge in alcohol. Even after his sister's death, he hadn't — knowing if he touched the stuff, it would start him in a spiral he didn't know if he could ever escape from. But he wasn't on duty tomorrow. And he could use a little numbness right now. Maybe it would knock some sense into his head.

He enjoyed the darkness tonight. Something about it seemed appropriate. Even the stars on the viewscreen seemed to suit the situation. They were copies of the originals, put on a screen for his enjoyment. The real thing was in the observatory, and he couldn't imagine facing that right now. No, the fact that they were fake and displayed for him seemed better.

He didn't deserve the real thing. Not after all he had done. And no, letting her go didn't even begin to make up for it.

Ram heard footsteps ring in the empty space out as someone came down the mess hall stairs. He nearly growled with annoyance when someone slid into the seat beside him.

"Does it look like I want company?" Ram asked, taking a sip of his drink.

"When have I ever cared about what you want?" Feingo asked.

Ram grunted.

They sat silent for a long moment, and the only sound that could be heard was the normal, soothing thrum of the ship's systems at work. Ram continued to stare at his cup, waiting for Feingo to take the hint and go away.

"You're missing your girl." It was a statement not a question.

Ram shot Feingo a look. "She wasn't *my* girl. The most I'll miss is having an extra set of hands to help with my duties," he said, deflecting.

Fengo laughed at that, clearly not buying it.

"Is that why you've dragged your feet at putting in a request for another captive?"

Ram slammed the glass down, splashing some of the liquid out onto the table. "I don't blasted *want* another captive."

Feingo held up his hands in mock surrender. "Sure, okay. No more captives. Got it."

If only the blasted fool did. Feigno was as stubborn as he was observant. It made him a pain at times, but also a good friend. He didn't back down if he knew he was right.

"Don't you have somewhere else to be?" Ram growled. "Someone else to bother?"

"Nope," Feingo said cheerfully. He pressed several buttons on the console in front of him, and a few moments later a drink appeared in the slot. "I drew the short straw on who of the squad had to come deal with your sulky ass."

"I'm not sulking."

Feingo let out a scoff. "Whatever, man. You just going to sit there and lie to me all night?"

"What do you want, Feingo?" Ram asked, suddenly weary.

"To help you."

"I don't need help."

"Lie all night it is," Feingo said with a chuckle, and took a swig of his own drink.

Ram shook his head, swirling his glass. They were both silent for some time. Finally, Ram said, "I was thinking about requesting a transfer to one of the exploration missions when we get back."

Feingo looked over at him in surprise. "Those are pretty high risk."

High risk wasn't the way Ram would put it, but it wasn't far off. Those missions were unlikely to return home in one lifetime. The plan was to go out to explore the far reaches of the solar system and beyond. They were equipped to sustain the crew for years and even, in theory, centuries of travel. Varus had only decided to fund a couple of them, but they were trying to find out more information about the galaxy around them. There were few records left of the original settlers who had come to Varus, but they had to come from somewhere.

"It'll be an adventure," Ram said, taking a drink.

"Or a whole lot of boring," Feingo said. "No guarantee they'll find anything. Or that you'll even still be alive by the time they do."

Ram shrugged. "It'll be a nice change of pace. I'm ready for something new."

"And what about your *not-yours* girl?"

He shouldn't even be thinking about Carina, but he couldn't stop the tumble of thoughts. Her golden hair, green eyes, sweet smile. Her quiet soothing company. Her snark, and hardworking attitude. The way she stirred such warm affection in him.

She was gone, but stars, he couldn't get her out of his head. He did miss her.

"Even if...*if*...I wanted to see her again, it's not like that's possible," he admitted. "Relations between us and Seutura are only going to worsen. It would take a blasted miracle to—" Ram broke off, shaking his head.

"Well, then," Feingo said, grabbing his glass. He clinked it against Ram's. "To miracles."

Chapter 30

The ground transport wove its way up the rough mountain road, carrying Carina and several other passengers toward the colony of Intrepid.

The first days back on Seutura had been chaotic. Their pilot had managed to land the stolen transport just on the outskirts of Osipenko city. They had immediately been taken to the capital for countless questions and interrogations.

No, I never saw their weapon systems.

No, I didn't have access to the command deck.

No, they didn't discuss strategy in front of us.

No, I didn't form any attachments.

The last one was a lie, she knew. She'd been attached. She shouldn't have been — should have kept her distance. But the deep ache in her spoke the truth.

The questions kept coming until they had squeezed every milliliter of information from the escaped prisoners. Only then, after almost an entire week, did they let them go. Of course, none of the prisoners' questions had been answered. Carina had explained, desperately, that they needed to help the other captives. Her pleas were met with political platitudes even she could see through. *Due to security reasons, the government officials can't disclose any information regarding the capture and subsequent negotiations. Information will be made available to the public at such time as it becomes necessary.* The official who had explained it to Carina sounded as though she were reading from a script, and there was no sincerity in her words.

Each of the escaped war prisoner's had been given a small stipend — "for their troubles" — and sent back to their respective provinces.

The crisp mountain air filled her lungs. Only a few kilometers more and they'd be home. Yeunay rode beside her and Pentil, a middle-aged man from the colony, sat a few seats away. He had been in one of the men's compartments that had been able participate in the escape. He had a wife and son back at Intrepid, but had barely talked about them or anything else on the way back.

"I'm sorry about Bryn," Yeunay said.

Carina nodded absentmindedly. That made the return bittersweet.

The only thing that made it bittersweet, she told herself. Although the thoughts felt empty even to herself.

Shaian had told her during the flight down that she'd found out Bryn was on the ship and which compartment she was being held in. She had done her best to get word to them, but at the time of escape, there had been no communication from that compartment.

Logically, of course, Carina knew the limitation of time that they had. The zero-g tunnel had taken longer than Shaian or the others had expected. It ended up being about half integrated prisoners and half from the prison sections that were able to escape. But that didn't make her feel any better. She felt a deep pit of anguish inside her — she walked free, while Bryn and so many others didn't. She should be happy that she was home — and she was, of course. But it was tempered with sorrow.

"We made it at least," Carina said. The words were hollow, but she said them for Yeunay.

Yeunay nodded. Even Pentil grunted. Rumor had it that he and his wife hadn't been getting along that well before the attack, but perhaps it was true that absence made the heart grow fonder.

"You can't blame yourself for surviving," Yeunay said. She apparently had realized Carina didn't believe her own words. "We're back. That's all we could do."

The conversation lapsed soon afterwards, and the rest of the transport ride passed in silence. Soon they were dropped off at the edge of the colony on the cracked concrete landing pad. They continued in silence as they walked through the worn streets to the housing area.

It was relatively quiet — most workers were in the mines at this time of day. She waved a greeting to the few residents she did see, though she only recognized one of them. They returned the distant greeting, but no one approached. She didn't know what she'd done if they had. Yeunay and Pentil seemed to have similar apprehensions.

Walking down the streets felt strange. It felt less familiar than she thought it should. She had been gone for seven weeks, but it shouldn't have changed as much as it had. They'd heard that since a good portion of their mining workforce had been taken, the Seuturan government had reassigned people up to the colony to make sure titanium mining didn't lag at all. But it wasn't just the people. Even the buildings felt strange. They were all exactly where they should be, but it was as if something was missing.

She would have to return to work tomorrow — Carina had been informed while she had still been in Osipenko city. Even Yeunay was told to report in the next day. Apparently the government had contacted all the places where the prisoners had gone missing and had already arranged for them to go back to work as soon as possible.

The three of them separated once they reached the housing area, saying awkward goodbyes to each other. The last bit she walked by herself. The metal steps up to her unit sounded especially loud in the dry air, and she entered her code on the keypad beside the door.

She stepped into her apartment, feeling an immense wave of both relief and sadness. The air was stale, and everything was covered in a thin layer of dust. The apartment seals were not enough to keep it out, and she normally had to clean two or three times a week to keep it neat.

Seven weeks. So short, but it felt like a lifetime.

She crossed the main room and went to the plant unit sitting on the small windowsill. Each of the small plants had withered. All that was left were dried up stalks with a few desiccated leaves attached.

Her fingers brushed over the leaves and stems, and they crumbled down into the dry soil below. She took a deep breath and felt the tears welling up. *What is happening to me? I'm home, I should be happy.*

The plants were replaceable. She could use the stipend — small though it was, compared to the pay she'd missed out on after not working for seven weeks — to buy more herbs.

But there was a cavernous hole in her chest. She was home. She had made it. But she wasn't complete. It wasn't just those she left behind, like Bryn, if she was being honest. A small part of her almost wished she had stayed.

It's his fault, she told herself. *That blasted barbarian. What am I even thinking?*

Ram had said she would want adventure. She still wasn't so sure, but she did want something. Someone, if she was being honest.

He had been hurting. His sister had died. It didn't excuse his behavior, but she found herself wishing that he had opened up more to her about it. Had given her enough time to understand and respond.

He was a soldier. Varusian. She had learned all that meant to him in the short time she had known him. She had come to realize his harshness had been for her sake as much as anything. He had been trying to protect her. Again, it didn't excuse what he did, but she came to understand it. There were far worse places to be on that ship than with Ram, and if she had caused enough trouble she could have been taken away from his charge.

And yet he had let her go so that she could return home — return to the sunlight. The words struck her even now. She had thought about them ever since he had said them.

Then why does everything feel so damn dark? she thought bitterly.

A knock on her door startled her, and she jerked back from the planter. Hope surged up in her, which she quickly squashed. How could she possibly hope for *that*?

She frowned and made her way to the door. Perhaps a neighbor had seen her come home and was checking on her. She keyed the door open. It slid open to reveal a man standing on the small step before her apartment.

"Oh. Hello Tennel," she said hesitating just a moment before giving him a small smile. She tried to hide her disappointment. She hadn't expected him at all. And, she realized guiltily, hadn't even thought to comm him. They didn't have an official understanding, but she probably should have at least sent a message letting him know she was safe and coming home.

He shifted slightly on his feet, looking her over. He was tall and lanky, with a mess of dark blonde hair atop his head that just brushed the collar of his worn jacket. His dark brown eyes didn't meet hers. "Heard you were coming home, and saw you arrive on the transport," he said.

"We just got back," she said, wrapping her arms around herself.

"Yeah." He cleared his throat. "You okay?"

She gave a little shrug. "I think so."

"Just wanted to say I, uh, don't mind," he said, eyes flicking around before landing back on her.

"Don't mind?" she echoed, trying to comprehend what he meant.

"Yeah. I mean, if you still want to get married," Tennel said. "I don't mind all that's...happened to you. It's okay."

Carina blinked, pulling her arms tighter to herself. She took a deep breath, thinking back to the awkward stares and waves she, Yeunay, and Pentil, had received on her way through the colony. It dawned on her that they would be viewed as *tainted*.

"I'm still me," she said, feeling slightly defensive.

"Of course," he said, giving her a small smile. But she had the uncomfortable feeling he didn't fully mean it. "So, if we want to get a contract to get married, then put in a request to transfer to Taneb we can." He reached and pulled something out of his pocket. It was a folded vellum print. He passed it to her. She reached out and took the paper with numb fingers. She skimmed it.

It was a half-filled marriage contract.

"Uh, this is...sudden," she said haltingly, eyes still searching the paper.

"Well, we've been talking about it for a while. And you got a stipend, which would help us get established." Her head shot up to look at Tennel, and he broke off, looking flustered. "I mean, I heard anyway. And uh, yeah, I figured life's short, right? Almost lost you forever."

A cold pit settled in her stomach. And suddenly it made sense. Tennel saw an opportunity. He'd heard she'd gotten a stipend — probably for an exaggerated amount, knowing how rumors traveled around here. And he'd wanted to ensure his chance didn't slip away.

She shouldn't be surprised. They had only talked of marriage in a strategic way after all. She knew that. Was fine with that. It was foolish that she had remotely expected anything different. Of course Tennel wouldn't care about her beyond her value as a strategic resource for him. It's what she expected and counted on. It made things less complicated that way.

She should be thrilled he didn't want to wait longer. That he didn't mind. It would give her the chance to get truly settled, move on to a better place and job. A new colony would help distance herself from her captivity and time with the Varusians. It would soon all fade away.

Carina opened her mouth to agree, but the words froze on her tongue. She couldn't. Perhaps she was more broken than she realized.

That blasted Barbarian.

"I'm sorry, Tennel," she found herself saying apologetically, reaching out to pass the contract back to him. "I think I need a little more time to settle back in here."

Tennel frowned down at the form as he took it back. "Well, I would like to know soon. If you're not interested, I talked to Krista about marriage when you were away. When I heard you were back, I wanted to try to make it work with you."

Carina blinked, and felt the absurd desire to laugh. Seven weeks and he had already proposed to someone else. And she knew he had only returned to her because of the stipend, not a motivation for Tennel to stick to his first commitment.

"That's okay."

He looked up at her, brow furrowed. "So, you sure?"

She felt an odd sort of peace fall over her. And an inexplicable loneliness. This was her chance to have what she always wanted.

"I'm sure, Tennel," she said, smiling softly. "Good luck to you."

Tennel turned and walked down the stairs. He didn't look back as he walked toward the center of town. If he had any regrets, it would only be for the missed stipend, she knew.

The clouds were rolling in. There was rarely rain, but when it did, it poured. It would be a dark afternoon, and a dark night. She stepped back inside, closing the hatch behind her. She leaned the back of her head against the door. Then, slowly, she sank to the floor, and deep sobs wracked her body. The darkness closed in around her.

If only there were stars, she thought. But in the rain there were no stars, and definitely no sunlight.

Chapter 31

Every muscle in her body ached as Carina made her way up the roughly hewn tunnels toward the exit of the mine shaft. It had been a rough day. Three of the mining machines had broken down, and they'd only had enough spare parts to repair two of them. She'd been assigned pickup duty today — her least favorite task that involved trailing behind the mining machines and picking up any ore they had missed. With the state the machines were in, there seemed to be more crumbled rock left behind than ended up in their carts. Her back ached from being hunched over all day, and her hands were raw from handling the rock and ore. The last year had felt extra hard on her body, as though those weeks away had changed something permanently in her.

She silently took the work slip the foreman passed her, shooting her a grateful smile, before continuing toward the main exit of the mine. On the plus side, she was one of the first one off her shift, since she'd finished her section early. And tomorrow was her day off.

She'd recently added a basil plant to her collection, in addition to the ones she'd had to replace in the last year, and wanted to try out a new bread recipe. It felt almost like a betrayal to think so, but food just didn't taste the same. It was bland, no matter the combinations she tried, and paled in comparison to the Varusian food she had enjoyed.

But still, she tried. Experimenting with different recipes and flavoring combinations — the ones she could get anyway. She'd share some with Giorgos, the older man who lived next door, and Yeunay.

Giorgos had been the only one not to care that they had been away for those weeks. He still treated them like they were Seuturan, and not tainted. Yeunay had started spending a lot of time with Girogos soon after they arrived, and they married a few months ago. Giorgos was getting close to needing to retire, but still stubbornly refused to take extra days off. He liked the work, he'd insisted. He was a good match for Yeunay. But Carina could see he was slowing down this last year. She'd started taking them bits of her cooking when she had the time.

Pentil had received a warm welcome from his wife and son when he got home. His son was especially happy. He was of working age, just a few more years before he would get a place of his own, but he seemed excited that his dad had come home. His wife was also excited, although that only lasted for a month or so. Absence had made the heart grow fonder, but it hadn't lasted.

As for Carina, she was content, she told herself, as she had many times before. She didn't mind being alone. Wasn't *really* alone in the community here. She was fine.

It had been nearly a year since they had come home. A year since she had been kidnapped as a hostage, and since she had escaped.

Her thoughts returned far too often — even more than she'd ever admit — to Ram, his twinkling eyes and charming smile. To the ship, the stars in the observatory, the beautiful little garden. The companionship she'd enjoyed. His laugh, and the way his eyes crinkled when he found her particularly amusing. It felt like a lifetime ago, like it was a completely different life. Like a dream she had woken up from.

It was foolish, she knew. She had been a prisoner of war. How could those weeks be better than the year since? She'd just had a little adventure. She would settle.

Tennel had married Krista just a month after Carina's conversation with him, and they had been approved for a transfer to another city not long after that. She hadn't been surprised, though it had stung her more than she'd thought it would. But she'd gotten over it.

Perhaps she was lonely. She didn't have many close friendships anymore. Bryn was gone, and she missed her friendship dearly, and most everyone else in the colony still treated her like she was a leper.

There was an awkward sort of distance with everyone, except Giorgos and Yeunay. Carina didn't know if it had to do with the fact that she'd been an enemy captive, or that she had come back when many others hadn't yet. She had hoped it would get better with time, but so far it hadn't. She had thought about requesting a transfer, though she knew it was likely to be denied. At least Giorgos didn't seem to care what the others thought.

She was just rounding the last corner of the dark path up to the surface exit when she saw movement in the shadows. Before she could cry out or pull away, a hand pressed firmly to her mouth and an arm wrapped around her body. Then she was dragged into the shadows.

Without hesitation she stamped down on the foot with the heel of her boot, never more thankful that she had decided to take Ram's advice and continue with self defense training. It shocked her attacker just enough for her to maneuver an elbow into his solar plexus and then a quick jab to the face, right where his nose should be. The jab missed its mark, hitting the attacker's cheek, but his grip had loosened enough for her to pull away. She turned to run and sucked in a breath to scream when she heard him speak.

"Nice moves, Buttercup. You've been practicing?"

Carina stumbled, skidding to a halt. She turned slowly, not believing her own ears. Her eyes met the ones she had most decidedly *not* been thinking about several minutes earlier.

He wore his light combat gear. It was different from the set he'd worn when they first met. She remembered him telling her about it one morning while they cleaned it. It was designed for movement and stealth more than raw defense, and it would have softened the blows she had dealt. Slipping from his grip must have been more from him being surprised than injured.

And he looked just as handsome as her fantasies remembered him. The same charming smirk, and eyes that held that mischievous twinkle. But there was a hint of wariness in his expression.

"What are you doing here?" she whispered fiercely, finally finding her voice. How had he gotten on planet? How had he found her? *Why* had he found her?

He had to get out of here before he got caught.

"Classified," he said, giving a small shrug. He wore the same grin as he had when he had first taken her through the null gravity tube on the *Architeuthis*. She scowled, giving one last look around before she tugged him deeper down the maintenance tunnel. There was more than one entrance into and out of the mines. Several maintenance hatches allowed for emergency access to different parts of the tunnels, but how could he have found one? She led him to the closest exit, out into the crisp mountain air. It was just fifty meters from the main exit, but it was shielded from view from where the other miners would be exiting soon and heading to the transport.

Only then did it dawn on her that she had put herself in a position where she was isolated with him. He gave no sign of discomfort at the blows she had dealt him. She remembered him telling her that a big part of defense was surprise, and using that get away. She had surprised him, but that wouldn't work again, and here she was, moving away from safety to be alone with him. But her first concern had been to make sure he didn't get caught.

"Does the word *classified* seem to impress the Varusian girls?" she asked. "So again — *what are you doing here?*" She emphasized each word.

"I'm not here for an attack or raid or anything, but I can't tell you anymore right now." He hesitated a moment longer. "I came to give you this."

He presented a small holostand, carefully holding it out for her to grab it.

She looked at, hesitating before taking it from his hand. It would have a message on it. But why would Ram be delivering a message?

She clicked a button on the holostand.

"Hi Carina," Bryn's voice said. A small image of her projected above the device. Just by looking at her, Carina could tell she was doing well. The way she held herself. The way her voice sounded. The way she smiled. "I wanted to say hi, and let you know everything is going fine..."

The message played for five minutes. Bryn talked about her journey to Varus, and life there. The first few months had been rough, but the integration plan had been designed to not leave the captives as mere captives. There were still some restrictions, but she was more like a citizen than not at this point. She still couldn't come home — she hinted that might change soon — but that in either case she didn't want to. In true Bryn fashion she had made the most of the opportunity, and had even met a guy that she was getting married to soon.

And if he hadn't been interested in her from the start, she probably convinced him by her sheer force of presence.

The message ended with a farewell, and a hope to see Carina sooner than later. Carina wiped tears from her eyes as it finished, and looked up at Ram. He was still standing there, uncertainty filling his face. She walked over to him, and reached up and kissed him on the cheek.

"Thank you," she whispered.

When she didn't immediately let go, his arms wrapped around her, and they held each other.

"I was originally going to just check in, maybe threaten that guy you said you were going to marry — let him know if he didn't treat you well, he'd hear from me, and then leave the message for you to find. But then, when I looked you up, I found out you'd never gotten married. So I just...came."

She pulled back to get a better look at him. She wanted to bury her head in his neck, breathe him in, and hold him all day.

"But you can't be here," she said, stepping away from him. "If you're caught..." she trailed off, and shook her head.

"It was important."

"*This* message was important?" she asked incredulously. He was risking his life to hand deliver a message. "Don't get me wrong. I'm thankful, but..."

"No, it was the other message that was important."

"What other message?"

He took out another holostand, but before she could grab it, he put it back away.

"It's so important that you're not letting me have it?"

"I was going to leave it for you, but now that you're here, I should just say it directly."

Her heart fluttered. He had come to give her a message from himself. And then anger rose in her.

"You were going to leave me a message without stopping and talking to me?" she said.

"Hey, I thought I was coming here to find *Mrs. Tennel*. I didn't want to disrupt her. I didn't expect you to not be married. But, since you're here..." He paused for a moment and took a deep breath, and then looked straight into her eyes. She could see the remorse on his face. "I'm sorry. I was an ass and an idiot. I was harsh because I...I was afraid. The possibility of losing you..." He shook his head.

"You're sorry for being harsh?" she asked. "What about for capturing me?"

Ram let out a laugh. "No, can't say I'm going to apologize for that one." He shrugged. "I *was* following orders. And it meant I got to meet you."

Carina scowled at him, trying to shove down the blasted butterflies that had decided to throw a party in her. She would *not* be charmed by him. "You disobeyed orders to chase me," she corrected him.

He smirked. "You're not wrong. Still, I can't bring myself to apologize for that."

"Well, your other apology is accepted." They stood there for a moment. She was unsure what else to say. Should she get going? She didn't want to leave, but if he was just delivering an apology...

"How's your garden?" he asked.

"Well, I finally replaced the plants that died while I was gone," she said.

"I'm sorry for that, too," Ram said, and she could hear genuine regret in his voice.

"I got a new one," she said, as if to make the time last longer. "Going to make a new bread recipe with it tomorrow."

"Sounds like something I'd like to try."

She looked at him. He seemed so unsure. But did he mean what he thought she meant?

Her heart stuttered, and she gazed back at him. Her mouth felt suddenly dry. She swallowed, licked her lips. "Ram—"

"Listen," he said softly. "Just say the word if you want me gone. I'll disappear, and you'll never see me again."

Gone? Now that he was here again? Was he crazy?

Am I crazy? I should scream for help. Report him. But that's the last thing I want.

"And what if I don't want you gone?" she asked, stepping towards him.

Ram's eyes lit up, a hopeful smile blooming on his lips. He took a step toward her, closing the distance, and reached his strong arms around her. She looked up at his face as her hands traced their way up his arms and then his shoulders and finally around his neck. One of his hands reached up and cupped the back of her neck. Their lips met in an explosion of warmth and comfort. She softened into the kiss, pressing herself against him. Her hands tightened on the top of his uniform. His scent, citrus and clove blended with him, surrounded her.

Sunlight entered her through that kiss. For the first time in a year she was not surrounded in darkness.

Too soon, they pulled apart. Ram's fingers rested on her cheek. She smiled up at him as his eyes traced over her face.

Reality hit her again.

"But now what?" she asked. It was the last thing she wanted to say, but how could this work? He was a Varusian soldier. They couldn't possibly have a future.

"Well," Ram said gently, bumping her chin so her gaze rose to meet hers. "I still have seven more years of service with Varus." Her heart sank, and her grip on his uniform tightened.

"Seven..." she said despairingly. "And then what? Stay here, hidden on enemy soil? What kind of life is that?"

His hands toyed with the strands of her hair near the back of her neck. "It'd be a life with you. What more could I want?"

"But seven years," Carian repeated. She was so close to happiness. Could she wait seven years? It was worth it, but she feared how much more she'd wither in the meantime.

"There's another option," Ram said, hesitation evident in his voice.

She looked at him. "What is it?"

"You could come to Varus," he said.

"And be your captive there?" she scoffed. But her heart soared. As many times as she'd thought of Ram in the past year, she had also often thought of Varus itself. To see the place Ram had spoken so fondly of. To see in person the sights from the pictures that had displayed in Ram's quarters. To possibly have a life better than this one.

"You wouldn't be a captive, or a prisoner or anything. You saw Bryn's message. It's true. We are trying to integrate the Seuturans into Varus society as much as possible." His eyes were hopeful, but were filled with apprehension at the same time. She couldn't bear to leave him like that. Things would not be perfect on Varus, she knew, but she'd be with him.

She reached up, hands touching his cheeks. "I think I'd like to see Varus," she said. "If you'll have me," she added, smiling softly up at him.

Ram's face broke into a grin. "Really? Are you sure?"

She scowled, but it wasn't in earnest. "Do you not want me to come back with you?" she asked, raising her eyebrows.

"Of course I do," he said, his hands trailing down to rest at her waist. "I just hadn't thought you'd want to. You seemed so hell-bent on being here."

"While I was a captive of a thick-headed barbarian," she said teasingly. Ram let out a short laugh. She took a deep breath. "I've…I've missed you, Ram. And while I could live here, I…" She took a breath. "I wouldn't mind a little adventure. Especially if it's with you."

Ram grinned, and drew her close for another kiss. She held him tightly, feeling contentment settle over her, sure and strong. Yes, this was where she was supposed to be. And she would revel in a little adventure if it meant staying by Ram's side.

"Hey Ram?"

"Mmm?"

"Did you happen to bring any cheesecake with you?"

Ram let out a laugh, and pulled her close, tucking her under his arm as he led her into the forest and toward a new life.

Acknowledgements

There are so many to thank who helped to bring this book into being. My beta readers who helped improve and shape this book. Carlee, my wonderful sister(-in-law) who managed to find time to help me edit during the insanity that is her wonderful life. My family, who were excited and encouraging every step of the way. My kids, who were just as excited as I was to see this book get finished. Tim, who has told me repeatedly that he "doesn't write romance novels," but nearly deserves to have his name on the cover with mine. Without him, this book would never have made it past the roughly jotted-down first draft in my notebook.

Free Novella - Continue the Story...

Bryn has found life as a Varus captive isn't terrible — but she's bored. When she's finally assigned to a Varusian, she hopes things are finally starting to get interesting. But Kaimen, the stoic soldier who is placed in charge of her, has made life even more stifling.

She gets more excitement than she bargained for when danger strikes, and she and Kaimen find they have to rely on each other to survive.

Sign up to get this free novella + book updates:
www.ellenrussell.com/free-novella

About the Author

Ellen Russell grew up listening to her mom read science fiction books to her, playing computer games, and planning out her own stories and worlds — and the beautiful dresses her heroines would wear.

Now she still loves a good book, games when she can, and finds time to dream up those worlds and ideas — and shamelessly doodles ideas on her to-do lists.

She lives in the Southern California desert with her geeky husband, five kids, and cuddly dog.

Get updates book updates from Ellen at
ellenrussell.com/newsletter

www.ingramcontent.com/pod-product-compliance
Lightning Source LLC
Chambersburg PA
CBHW021008180726
47993CB00019B/2000